D0995380

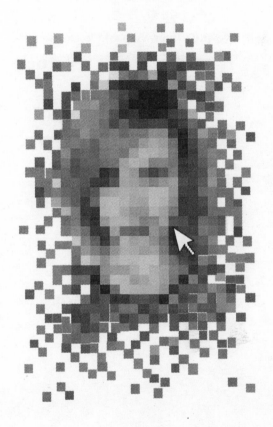

79 770 872 9

Also by Nicola Doherty

Love and Other Man-Made Disasters

For older readers

The Out of Office Girl
If I Could Turn Back Time
Girls on Tour

Lola Offline

nicola Doherty

Orion

ORION CHILDREN'S BOOKS

First published in Great Britain in 2017
by Hodder and Stoughton

1 3 5 7 9 10 8 6 4 2

Text © Nicola Doherty, 2017

The moral right of the author has been asserted.

A CIP catalogue record for this book
is available from the British Library.

ISBN 978 1 5101 0051 0

Printed and bound in Great Britain
by CPI Group (UK) Ltd, Croydon, CR0 4YY

The paper and board used in this book are made
from wood from responsible sources.

MIX
Paper from
responsible sources
FSC® C104740

Orion Children's Books
An imprint of
Hachette Children's Group
Part of Hodder and Stoughton
Carmelite House
50 Victoria Embankment
London EC4Y 0DZ

An Hachette UK Company
www.hachette.co.uk
www.hachettechildrens.co.uk

To Alex

My impulse was to pick him up by the scruff of his hoody and ping him out of my room, but I was trying to be less impulsive. Since that was what got me into trouble in the first place.

'Fine,' I said. 'Have it. Just clear out when I come home, and *don't* use my sheets.'

Lenny's mouth dropped into a startled O. With a pang, I realised he hadn't just wanted to get under my skin; he'd wanted me to react to him. Maybe it was his weird way of showing he would miss me.

'Seriously, Len,' I said. 'Be my *guest*.' I gave him a hug, normally a guaranteed way of getting rid of him. Instead he started doing parkour around my room, until Mum shooed him out. That was typical Lenny; he recovered quickly. At least I didn't have to worry about him.

'Hey!' Dad said, appearing in the doorway. 'So . . . you're doing your packing.'

'Yep.' I nodded, mirroring his awkward smile.

'Great.'

Most of my chats with Dad in the past few months had followed this pattern.

'So . . . you're having your breakfast.'

'Yep.'

'Great.'

Awkward smiles. Silence.

To try and spice things up, I added, 'I don't think it will be that cold in Paris, but I'm not sure.'

He took out his phone, relieved to have a distraction. 'Siri! Check weather in Paris in February.'

Dad was so devoted to Siri, I was surprised he hadn't

included her in our family conference. He obviously found her much easier to talk to than me.

'I'm sorry, I didn't get that,' said Siri.

'Siri!' Dad barked. 'Check! Weather! In Paris!'

'OK. Checking for you now,' said Siri.

'Shouldn't you say please?' said Mum.

'Why on earth would I say please? It's a robot.'

'Shh!' said Mum. 'She'll hear you.'

I cleared my throat. 'Mum. Dad. I've decided something else.'

They both turned to me, with the identical worried expressions that had become so familiar.

'I'm changing my name. To Lola.'

'But why—' Mum said, before closing her mouth. She knew why.

'Are you sure the school will let you change your name?' Dad said.

'You saw the form they sent – child's name, child prefers to be known as. Lola is sort of a nickname for Delilah. And I can use your surname,' I added, to Mum.

'Lola Maxwell – not bad,' said Dad.

'Lola is awful! It sounds like a stripper,' said Mum. *Unlike Delilah*? I thought. 'Surely we can think of something better.' Now she and Dad both had their phones out.

'Siri! Suggestions for girls' names!'

'OK. Checking for you now.'

Dad looked up. 'What about your middle name?' he said hopefully.

'Dad!' 'Steve!' Mum and I said in unison. My middle name is Uhura. What can I say? Dad is a *Star Trek* fan.

Not the Next Generation, and definitely not the films, just the original series which . . . Never mind. It's too boring.

'Look, darling, if you want you can call yourself Lola,' Mum said quickly. 'Just for this year. But you can't change it forever, you know.'

I wanted to tell her it *was* forever – but something stopped me. Maybe it was the sight of the new lines around Mum's eyes despite all the organic skin cream she bought, or the fact that Dad's fingers were always drumming nervously these days, when he wasn't talking to Siri.

They didn't have the option of moving to Paris, or changing their names. My parents weren't international people of mystery; they were a worried-looking PR exec and IT consultant. Although, my dad had recently made a lot of money from an app – hence they were able to afford Paris.

A lump was growing in my throat as I thought how much I was going to miss them. And how ashamed I was that I had done this to them.

I looked around my room, crammed with the junk of years: all my books, from *Babysitter's Club* to Jane Austen, my ancient *Keep Calm* poster, my bean bag collapsing in front of my laptop and Flossie, my pink flamingo light. It was going to take a while to clear it all out for Lenny, but I would do it. I'd erase every trace of myself and their lives would be a whole lot easier.

Chapter three

By now, I'm sure you're wondering what it was, exactly, that I did. Don't worry. This isn't going to be one of those times where you wait until you're 90% through and then find out I stole a traffic cone or something. I will tell you, and soon. But here's what I didn't do.

1. It was nothing sexual (I wish. The closest I've come to sending a sexy picture was when I had to email the dermatologist a picture of my mole.)
2. I didn't kill a lion.
3. Or put a cat in a bin.
4. I didn't hurt anyone. At least not physically.
5. I didn't break any laws.
6. I just made a stupid mistake.

And now I was paying for it. Every day I regretted it; I feel horrible and worthless and a pathetic excuse of a person. I wished I was anybody but me. But maybe that wish was about to come true.

8

Chapter four

As the taxi slid along the Parisian boulevards, I examined my hair in the mirror app on my phone. I'd cut it in a bob and dyed it peroxide pinky-grey. It was way more edgy than anything I'd previously attempted and I really wasn't sure if I could pull it off. I looked like an old lady with really good skin.

'It looks fine, love,' Mum said, beside me.

She'd been really nice about my hair – saying I'd done a good job on it except for the very back, and taking me to her hairdresser's to sort it out. Dad said, 'So . . . you've changed your hair.' Lenny just said, 'Vletu' – which meant 'Freaky' in Delilish.

I didn't care. My main aim was to look different from *that* photo. The one all the articles had used, the one that came up in Google searches, where my long dark hair was flipped over one shoulder and I was smiling that awful smile. My heart started to race again at the thought of it. *It's OK*, I told myself. *That wasn't me. I'm Lola Maxwell.*

'I think we're here,' Mum said. 'Rue Bonaparte.'

Of course my new school was on rue Bonaparte. Rue Baguette or rue Sacré Bleu would be too much of a cliché.

'Yes, this is it,' said the driver. He spoke excellent English – as did the people in our hotel and in the restaurant last night. At this rate, it would be easier to learn Tagalog.

Like everything in Paris, the Jean Monnet International School was beautiful. With its high stone walls, and array of flags flying outside, it looked more like a museum or an embassy than a school. Kids of all ages were standing outside chatting in groups. Most of them were in jeans and jumpers, like me, but somehow theirs seemed so much more stylish. My hands were suddenly very cold.

'Come on, Delilah,' Mum said, tucking her arm in mine. 'It'll be fine.'

'Lola,' I hissed instantly.

'Really?' Mum looked distraught.

'Yes! That way I won't slip up. I mean, I'll get used to it.'

A million different expressions seemed to pass across Mum's face before she plastered on her professional smile. 'Of course, darling,' she said.

We went inside, towards the glass-walled office on the left. Beyond, I got a glimpse of a courtyard, with three leafless chestnut trees rising out of pale gravel. I'd seen those trees so often on the school's website, it was strange to see them in real life.

A tall, dark boy was coming out of the office just as we were coming in. Seeing us, he held the door open, and stood back to let us in. But we were standing back to let

10

him *out*. We all performed an awkward little dance together until he said, 'Please! After you,' and waved us through. While all this was happening I took a quick survey. Dimples and brilliant green eyes. Dark skin, Asian, nice smile. He was dressed like no teenage boy I'd ever seen, with a trench coat over a jumper over a buttoned-up shirt, and a leather satchel over one shoulder.

'Thank you!' said Mum. 'I mean, *merci beaucoup*.'

'No problem,' he said. 'Cool hair, by the way,' he added, to me.

'Thanks!' I said, startled. Doors held open and a random compliment from a stranger? I could see why people liked Paris.

Chapter five

The school secretary, Pauline, was nice and friendly: yet another French person with excellent English.

'Now, if I could just have a photocopy of your passport,' she said.

I knew this was coming but it was still very scary, handing it over. There was every chance that she'd recognise my name. Thankfully, she barely glanced at it as she copied it and returned to my forms.

'Well, Lola Maxwell, welcome to Jean Monnet! Let's give you a quick tour.'

Although the building must have been two hundred years old, it was state of the art, from the classrooms equipped with video-conferencing to the espresso machines. Espresso machines! It was all a bit different from my old school with its freezing prefabs, scarred parquet floors and eternal smell of lamb hotpot from the canteen.

Pauline said, 'Now, I will hand you over to one of our students – she's in your year group. She'll be your student mentor – show you your accommodation, show you around generally. Oh, here she is!'

The new arrival didn't so much enter the room as vault in, dressed head to toe in workout gear, blonde ponytail flying.

'Hey!!!' she said, or rather sang in an American accent, brown eyes shining. 'How *are* you? It's so nice to *meet* you! I'm Fletcher!!'

'Hi. I'm Lola.'

'Lola! *Welcome*! So how do you like Paris?'

I gave her a world-weary smile. 'Oh, you know. It's a bit of a dump, isn't it?'

A look of total bafflement crossed her face.

'Sorry,' I said, feeling bad. 'I was just joking. Paris is beautiful.' People often didn't get my jokes; I was too deadpan, apparently. Or maybe they just weren't any good.

'That's funny!' I thought Fletcher couldn't smile any harder, but I was wrong. 'OK. Let's show you your room!'

The student accommodation was on the top floor of the building, overlooking the central courtyard. Fletcher explained, as she guided us upstairs, that most students lived with their parents, with just a small number of senior students living in.

'So we're like a *very* exclusive club!' she said. 'It's going to be awesome to have you. We need more ladies around here!'

I just nodded, feeling too out of breath to reply; this was like doing step aerobics.

'These stairs are a good workout, huh?' she said, beaming at us. 'A few more weeks and you'll have

13

buns of steel! This is the girls' corridor – the boys are on the opposite side, and the teaching assistants are in between,' she added, obviously to reassure Mum. 'This is my room . . .' she added, as we passed a door covered with photos and inspirational quotes like 'Make Today Ridiculously Amazing!' and '#Eat Clean, #Train Dirty!'

'Here we are!' she said, unlocking the door to my room.

It was as tiny as a prison cell, with a narrow bed and a low attic ceiling. A tall, narrow window overlooked the courtyard. From the bed, you could reach out and touch the opposite side of the desk. And that was about it, aside from a fun-sized wardrobe. Where did all the fashionistas downstairs keep their Louboutins? Oh, yes. They lived at home.

'What do you think, um, Lola?' Mum said. 'It's nice, isn't it? Cosy.'

Cosy! Mum would have made a great estate agent.

'It's great,' I said, hoping I wouldn't cry.

'It's pretty small! I know. But look, from your window you can see . . .' Fletcher went over to open it, leaning out and displaying a perfectly toned rear end. I couldn't help but stare at it, then felt like a pervert.

'Oh – sorry!' she said. 'I thought you could see the Eiffel Tower. You can from my room, though. Wanna come see?'

'Maybe later, thanks,' I said. I didn't want to sound unfriendly, but I had to cut this short before the tears came.

14

'OK. Well, come and holler if you get bored!' She mimed knocking. 'A bunch of us are going for fro-yo later, you should come!'

As soon as she had gone, Mum turned to me and said, right on cue, 'She seems lovely!'

'Yeah,' I said, sitting down. 'I'm sure we'll be BFFs before long.' Sarcasm seemed the best way to make sure I didn't break down entirely.

'Come on, love,' she said briskly. 'Let's get your stuff from downstairs.'

'OK,' I said. I was glad she'd been brisk. If she'd been nice, I would definitely have howled.

'Do you want me to help you unpack?' Mum said, once we had got everything upstairs with the help of a passing teaching assistant.

I shook my head, assuming she would ignore me and stay anyway to help arrange all my shoes in the right order.

But she didn't.

'All right then, sweetie,' she said, pulling me in for a hug. 'Let's talk soon, OK? We can Skype whenever you want. Every day. And it's only a month to Easter.'

One. Month. By myself. In Paris. And then another two months and potentially another year. How had I got myself into this situation?

'It's going to be absolutely fantastic, De-Lola,' Mum said, again. 'They are all going to love you. Studying in Paris – what an opportunity!'

I nodded half-heartedly. I was used to these positive press releases from Mum.

'I just . . . I do feel bad about the money,' I said, awkwardly. 'I know we've talked about this but . . . the fees here. . .'

Mum just shook her head. 'That's what Eat Easy is for!' she said.

Eat Easy was Dad's app. It allowed you to place an order with any takeaway, without having to phone up. The irony wasn't lost on me that Dad had made a lot of money by inventing a technology that meant you didn't have to talk to people.

We hugged one last time, and then she left. I leaned forward out of my mousehole window to see her cross the courtyard, but I couldn't see anything. Panicked, I dodged back and forth and up and down, feeling superstitiously that if I couldn't see her now, I would never see her again. Finally, I had a glimpse of her back, and then she was gone.

Straight away, I reached for my phone. I needed to feel connected to the world. I needed to see what Jules was up to on Instagram, or read Ellie's tumblr, or watch Nisha do one of her make-up haul videos. I wouldn't contact them, of course – I just wanted to watch.

But there was no internet on this floor. No WiFi networks listed at all. In any case – more to the point – I had closed all my accounts. And I was sick of stalking them. It was time to start a new life, alone, in Paris.

Another impulsive decision I was starting to regret.

Chapter six

My first thought, the next morning, was that there was absolutely no way I could leave my room and go down to breakfast.

My second thought was that I had nothing to wear. The thing about wearing a uniform every day is that you don't get the chance to develop any sense of style. And I wasn't even sure what my style should be. Was I preppy? Alternative? Classic? I had no idea.

These were the ten things I knew about myself:

1. I definitely wasn't cool.
2. I was a Ravenclaw, a feminist and a prefect.
3. I liked languages and politics, but also Jane Austen and sit-coms and stationery.
4. I loved the idea of baking, but I was terrible at it. My one attempt at a cake came out looking like a crater on the moon.
5. I was outspoken and idealistic. I always had my hand up in class.
6. I was also impulsive. And I had a bad habit of saying

stupid things and making jokes that weren't funny whenever I felt nervous.

7. I wasn't sporty, though it was technically true what I'd said on my practice UCAS form – that I'd 'represented my school at basketball' (once, on the D team).

8. I wasn't great at make-up beyond the basics, and I was clueless about fashion.

9. I knew nothing about drugs. I had been drunk on vodka and coke, and it was fun though I didn't want to do it every night.

10. I wouldn't have minded meeting more boys – or any boys.

That was who I used to be, anyway. But who was I now? Did I have to be completely different now that I was Lola? If so, how would I even manage that? There was no sorting hat here to tell me where I belonged at Jean Monnet.

I was having a full-on existential crisis, and it wasn't even eight a.m.

'Breathe!' I muttered, looking at myself in the mirror. Finally, after trying on and rejecting my entire wardrobe, I settled on my black jeans and a denim shirt. I spent ages trying to do my make-up with shaking hands. Breakfast with strangers. Nobody to sit with. How would Lola cope?

Simple. She wouldn't. She would sneak out, and try and grab a pastry at a café instead.

At least, that was the plan until I ran into Fletcher, just outside my room.

'Heyyyyyyy, Lola!' she said, managing to get about five syllables out of the word. 'There you are! I was just coming to grab you for breakfast.'

I was grateful to her, genuinely. But I found it hard to relate to her lively chatter about the 'awesome run' she'd been on and how pretty the spring bulbs were.

'Do you run?' she asked, as we reached the bottom of the stairs.

'Um, no,' I said. 'I'm not a runner. I've tried, but it nearly killed me.'

'I was the exact same! You just need to start slow. But there are a ton of other groups, if running's not your jam. We've got debate, art, Culture Vultures, a really great church group . . .'

Uh-oh. For the first time I noticed the little silver crucifix at her neck. Not that there was anything wrong with religion, but . . . it wasn't for me. Or Lola.

The cafeteria was really nice by any standards, let alone school. Orange chairs were grouped around round wooden tables, and long white counters were laden with pastries, fruit and bread.

But what really caught my eye were the boys. Boys, left, right and centre. Walking around, having breakfast, chatting. After an all-girls school, it was pretty bewildering. How was I ever going to get any work done?

'So I try to walk *right by* these bad boys,' Fletcher was saying.

I jumped, thinking she had noticed me staring. But she was nodding towards the glossy pastries. 'I actually have a blender in my room, and a fridge. I do these kale and almond smoothies that are totally delish. You should stop by for one some time!'

A *kale smoothie*? Was she trying to kill me?

'So help yourself – and then come join us! My friends are sitting over there – that's my boyfriend, Hunter, in the green sweater.'

Her boyfriend looked like the cruel jock who beat up the sensitive gay guy in every American teen film. Beside him were two other identical perfect couples, all ultra-white teeth and Abercrombie clothes. Wherever I fitted in, it wasn't with them. And I was sure that Fletcher didn't want me joining them, not really; she was just doing her duty. So it was *my* duty to stay away from them – for her sake as much as mine.

'Thanks,' I said awkwardly. 'I'll just ... I'm having trouble choosing. Don't wait for me.'

'Sure. I better move away from these ... Get thee behind me Satan!' She held up crossed fingers at the pastries, laughing, and bounced off.

As I loaded up my plate with croissants, I caught the eye of a girl standing behind me.

'Do you think if she actually met Satan,' she said, deadpan, 'she'd try and spread butter and jam on him?'

I snorted with laughter.

'Cool hair, by the way,' said the girl.

'Thanks!' Hers was dyed too – a heavy jet black with one purple streak, pinned up in a mass of wild curls. Her nose was pierced, her brown eyes were world-weary and she was wearing a faded long-sleeved purple T-shirt under denim dungarees. I didn't think she was the kind of person who would normally want to be my friend. Maybe my new hair was making me look a lot cooler than I actually was.

As she moved her tray along, I desperately tried to think of something witty to continue our conversation. 'So . . . if I'm not having a kale smoothie, what beverages do you recommend?' Then kicked myself. *Beverages?* What did I sound like?

'Coffee. Lots of it. Only way I'm getting through IB One.'

IB One; the first year of the International Baccalaureate – the equivalent of Year Twelve. That meant she was a year younger than me, but she seemed much older.

'Oh, you're in the same year as me.'

'Then I'll try and debrief you. Unless you have plans with the Young Republicans over there?' she said.

'No plans,' I said. We headed towards the till, and as we walked by Fletcher's table I gave her an apologetic nod. 'Just going to catch up with . . .' I mumbled.

'No problem!' Fletcher said. Her friends didn't seem to care, but she looked disappointed and I felt like a heel. Still, I told myself, it was for the best.

Chapter seven

'My name's Vee, by the way,' said my new friend. 'Have you got your meal card? You just swipe it, like this.'

'Lola.' I copied her, relieved that I had someone to show me – and that I managed it without an embarrassing fuss.

'So when did your dad start his new job?' Vee asked, as we took our seat at an empty table.

'Um – he hasn't.' Not unless you counted a new IT contract in Winchelsea.

'Your MOTHER? Oh my God! I have never *ever* heard of someone moving because of their mother's job. That is so cool! I have to tweet this.'

She pulled out her phone; I shrank away instinctively. I really hated to disappoint Vee, but I had to come clean.

'It wasn't either of my parents' jobs. I'm here on my own.'

'You're *so* lucky. I wish I boarded.' She gazed at me wistfully, still clutching her phone. 'Let me add you on Twitter. What's your handle?'

'I'm not on it.'

'Snapchat? Instagram? Whatsapp?'

'Nope. None of them.'

She stared at me, open-mouthed.

'*Nothing?* Are you Amish or something?'

I faked a laugh despite my rising heart rate. 'Nope. Just taking a technology break.'

'But you have email, right?' asked Vee. 'Or will you be sending all your homework in by owl?' She grinned at me, and I grinned back, relieved that she wasn't going to push it.

'Well. Since you can't stalk everyone online . . . Want me to kick it old-school, and explain to you who everyone is?' she said.

'Oh, God, yes. Please.'

'Let's see. You've already met the Americans.' Her eyes flickered to Fletcher. 'Every Sunday they go to the American Church and then to get frozen yoghurt, or Baskin-Robbins if they're feeling really crazy, and then they go and do glow yoga. I mean the girls do yoga, the boys play lacrosse. They're a bunch of basics. Paris is wasted on them.'

'OK,' I said, laughing. I wouldn't want to get on her bad side, but Vee was entertaining.

'Then there are the computer geeks . . . At least they used to be geeks but now we've all grown up, we've realised they're actually kind of cool. Over there, see that table where they've all got their laptops out?' I nodded.

'Then we've got the Diplobrats,' she went on, indicating a group of preppy-looking boys and girls. 'They're all terribly international – speak about five languages each,

23

and all want to be politicians. They run the Monnet Mail – that's our online newsletter – and the Student Council and they're all off to Harvard and Cambridge. They're not bad people, they're just . . . exhausting.'

'OK.' I decided not to mention that in my previous life, I was arts editor of our school newspaper, *and* I spoke five languages.

The group all turned round as a tall boy approached them, and a couple of them held up their hands for high-fives. It was the same boy who'd held the door open for me the other day. He was in another crisp shirt, grey this time.

'I met that guy already,' I said.

'Oh, that's Tariq Pirzada. Our future president of the Student Council,' said Vee. 'He goes out with Priscilla Adeboye. They're both our Grade Representatives this year.'

'Is that like a prefect?'

'Yeah. Just more self-important.'

Ouch. Looking over at the group, I remembered how excited I was to be prefect – sitting on committees and bringing people's problems to the staff. Lenny said all the power went to my head. But I asked him: would he have said the same thing if I'd been a boy? With a pang, I wondered if Lenny was missing me, or turning into a sexist monster without me. Who would bother to raise his consciousness now?

'The whole Grade Rep system is ridiculous. They're basically unpaid stooges for the teachers,' Vee was saying. 'I can't imagine why anyone would want that, can you?'

'I – no, not really.'

I would have loved to know how the Grade Reps were selected, how long their tenure lasted and what their responsibilities were, but I wanted Vee to like me more. 'Which one is Priscilla?' I asked, just to say something.

'She's at the end – see, the black girl in the white shirt, with the suede skirt . . .'

I saw the girl she meant: tall and pretty, with queenly braids piled high on her head. She and Tariq looked as if they were friends as well as being a couple. Vee continued, 'Her dad works for a massive oil company. She's also going to be president of something. In a couple of years, I'm sure they'll all be in the White House, dropping bombs on some village.'

I looked back at Tariq, who was eating a yoghurt. He didn't look particularly violent. I wondered what Vee had against them all.

'That sort of covers it as far as our year group is concerned,' Vee said, waving her coffee cup around. 'Everyone else is just sort of normal. I do have friends by the way – they're just not big breakfast eaters.' An alert was ringing on her phone. 'Time for class. What have you got first? Classical Greek and Roman Studies? How retro. Hopefully we'll have some classes together though.'

'Yes!' I was so happy I'd met Vee. Of course, at this stage I probably would have made friends with a serial killer, but I was really flattered that someone so cool and interesting was talking to me. It was early days of course – but it looked as if I just *might* have made my first friend here.

Chapter eight

As soon as I left Vee, though, I was plunged into a world of strangers again. By the time we were five minutes into Classical Greek and Roman Literature, it was clear that the standard was frighteningly high. We were reading a passage from the *Iliad*. I was pleased that I'd read the book in advance; Priscilla Adeboye, who was sitting near me, had read parts of it in the original Greek. Even the classroom was intimidating; with its high ceilings and elaborate plasterwork, it looked like a place for dukes and duchesses to meet for salons – not clueless teens on the run.

At least the teacher, Mr Gerardo, was nice: young and friendly, pacing enthusiastically around the room as he spoke. With his thinning hair and flowery shirt, he looked like a Hollywood casting director's idea of a classics teacher. He wasn't actually wearing a bow tie, but he definitely looked as if he owned one.

'The other thing you need to decide, quite soon, is the topic of your extended essay,' he said, towards the end of class. 'Does anyone want to kick around some ideas?'

'Could I write mine on Achilles and Patroclus?' asked one boy.

'Yes, great idea. Lots to talk about there including comradeship, cowardice, homoeroticism even,' he said. 'Anyone else? It doesn't have to be something we've studied. You can pick anything from the classical world – like Plato's *Symposium*, or Ovid's love poems . . .'

I was scared enough that everyone seemed to know exactly what those were, when beside me Priscilla said, 'What about the Delphic Oracle?'

'Yes, that could be interesting, Priscilla,' Mr Gerardo said, sitting on the edge of his desk. 'Do you want to tell the others who that was?'

'She was a priestess, based at the shrine of Delphi, who was said to speak with the voice of Apollo. She was always an older woman, given the name of Pythia, and kings and so on would come to consult with her,' Priscilla said.

'Why are you drawn to that in particular?'

'I like the idea that the most influential voice in the Greek world was a woman's.'

OK; whatever Vee said, Priscilla was pretty cool – the kind of person I wanted to be when I grew up. I also admired her style: crisp white shirt, cardigan and little suede skirt. I looked away so she wouldn't see me fangirling all over her.

'Yes! Excellent point!' Mr Gerardo said again. I loved how enthusiastic he was. 'You could also explore the Delphic maxims . . . A list of sayings, supposedly from

27

Apollo himself. There's one very famous one – does anyone know it?'

How on earth were we supposed to know that?

'Is it *Be Yourself*?' Priscilla asked, frowning.

'Close,' said Mr Gerardo. 'It's *Know Thyself*. Which is an interesting difference, isn't it?

'When you come to read *Hamlet*, you'll hear Polonius say "to thine own self be true". But for the Greeks, it was more important to *know* yourself. Which do we think is more important?'

I had promised myself that I wouldn't raise my hand too much, or talk in class as much as I used to. I didn't want to draw attention to myself. But nobody else was saying anything. So I said, 'Know yourself. Because you can't be yourself . . . Until you *know* who that is.'

'Yes!' said Mr Gerardo. 'Exactly, Lola.' He beamed.

I felt like a fraud: I might have been able to answer that question but it didn't mean that I really knew myself, or knew who the hell I was supposed to be these days. But still, I left feeling that at least there was one class I was definitely going to enjoy.

After that I had a session with a teaching mentor to help me get up to speed with all the coursework. Her name was Ms Tennant and she was almost disturbingly empathic, mirroring all my expressions with a scary intensity.

'So how is it all *going* so far?' she said.

'It's going OK – I mean I won't know for another week or so.'

'Of course. But it still must be *very* stressful.'

I nodded, trying to look as if I was a normal student agonising over coursework and exams, rather than a fugitive from internet justice.

Then I looked up. Was she being ... a bit *too* empathic? Did she *know*?

It was possible. The teachers would presumably have access to my forms that had my real name on them. Just two seconds on Google would give them the entire story.

'I'm fine,' I muttered.

'OK,' she said. 'Well, any problems you can speak to your pastoral Head of Year. That's Mr Gerardo.'

That was a relief, at least. We discussed the rest of my subjects: English Literature, French, Standard Level Maths and Standard Level Biology. For Group Six, I wanted to take Mandarin, but Ms Tennant had other ideas.

'You're already very language-heavy,' she said. 'Even for your Group Three, you should really be doing something like History or Philosophy – instead of Classical Greek and Roman Literature. How about dropping CGRL and doing History instead?'

'No, no,' I said, panicked. I definitely didn't want to give that up.

'We do want you to broaden out – that's what the IB is all about. Get out of your comfort zone. What about Computer Science?'

I was already feeling thoroughly out of my comfort zone, so we compromised with me doing History as a Group Six subject. My heart sank at the thought of all the extra work.

'What about the community service module?' I asked.

'I think you have enough on your plate. My recommendation is that you start that up next year.'

'But won't it be too late?' I was crushed. That was one of the things that had attracted me most about the IB; the fact that you had to do voluntary work as part of it.

'Lola,' she said. 'The IB is very demanding – even for people who aren't joining in the middle of term. That's why we recommended to you and your parents that you not do the full Diploma. You can just get the IB certificate, which is a great qualification in itself.'

I left her office feeling very deflated. If I'd stuck with A-Levels, I would be doing the things I was good at – languages. But now I was being stretched across a ton of things I didn't know if I could do, or wanted to. How was I going to manage it all?

Now it was lunch time: another ordeal. I made my way through the crowd towards the cafeteria. I could see Vee ahead of me, talking to a few other people. They looked far, far cooler than me; one of the boys was wearing actual leather trousers.

I knew I should just go up and talk to them. But I was worn out after a morning of unfamiliar things. Also, what if I was pushing in where I wasn't wanted? Vee had been friendly, but what if her friends didn't want to talk to the new girl?

I slunk back across the courtyard, keeping my head down, and then out past reception.

Chapter nine

Unlike my old school, the place was minimum-security – once I showed my student ID, which said I was IB level, I was allowed out.

As I walked along the street, I tried to cheer myself up by thinking: I'm in *Paris*. I turned right out of the school, and within minutes I was beside a huge park, with tall black gold-topped railings and trees, bare against the cold blue February sky. I knew, from my pre-arrival research, that this was the Jardin du Luxembourg.

I was surrounded by beauty. On one side was the park: on the other side, little cafés with people sitting outside, chatting and drinking espresso, wearing scarves and sunglasses. There was something about Paris that made it more than fine to wander around on your own. I wasn't escaping; I was exploring.

I was also hungry. But could I really walk into one of these cafes and eat by myself? Surely I would look like a loser. But I couldn't go back to school either.

After passing several expensive restaurants, I found a more modest place, where I sat in a corner inside. I ordered a Coke and a croque-monsieur, which I knew was an extra-delicious ham and cheese toastie.

'*Merci,*' I said, as the waiter gave me my Coke. I had a feeling this place was expensive, but it didn't matter. I had a pretty good allowance.

There were so many reasons to be grateful. I had a good allowance. I was in Paris. I had escaped. But I was so unhappy, I could barely eat my croque-monsieur. The loneliness felt like a vice gripping my chest, slowly killing me. What was I *doing* here? It would have been hard to go back to my old school, but at least I knew everyone. Here, I was like an alien. If I vaporised back to my space ship, nobody would notice. Vee seemed friendly enough – but she already had friends.

Opposite me, two older women were having a glass of wine with their lunch. It was obviously the done thing here. Pity I couldn't have one.

Then I thought about it. Obviously, it wasn't something I would ever do in my normal life. But I was in Paris now: this was my chance to do something completely different. Why not? Maybe this was the kind of thing Lola would do, if not Delilah. I started picturing my new self: a cool, hardbitten girl who kept a bottle of whisky in her room and poured a tot of it on stressful days. On the spur of the moment, I ordered one too.

I took a sip. It certainly *seemed* to help with the tight, horrible feeling. With a glass of wine in hand, I felt less like a clueless teenager and more like a chic Parisienne. As I sipped and munched, I began to feel better, and soon my glass was empty.

'*Voulez-vous un autre verre?*' the waiter asked.

'*Oui, merci,*' I said, before I realised exactly what he was saying. Before I could correct my mistake, he'd brought me another glass.

I must look older than I was – maybe it was the white hair? It was too late, and too embarrassing, to say no. I found myself sipping it. Then I saw the time, and drank it down in a panic.

After leaving a one-euro tip though I had no idea if that was right, I started heading back towards the school. It was close by; I had time.

Or at least, I would have if I hadn't got lost.

I was just around the corner – so why couldn't I find it? I didn't have data so no Google Maps. And I was horribly fuzzy from the wine; I couldn't believe how quickly it had gone to my head. Oh; and now it was raining.

'Hey!' said a voice, just behind me.

I looked round and it was him again: Tariq.

'You go to Jean Monnet, don't you?' he said. 'Here – have some umbrella.'

I couldn't believe how secure he was – straight-out admitting that he recognised me. Most boys I knew would never have admitted to recognising a girl even in an ID parade. But he was different – with his golf umbrella and his polished shoes. His accent was the kind of cut-glass posh English that reminded me of old films.

'Thanks. I was a little lost,' I admitted. Oh no. Did I just say 'losht'?

'No problem. I was just coming back from the print-er's,' he said, lifting a white plastic bag. 'Picking up some flyers for the Film Club. What about you? Prison break?'

'What? Oh, no. I was . . . Meeting a . . . my godmother for lunch.' Where did that come from? 'I was trying to nag – nagivate by that pharmacy, but that's a different one. God, there're pharmacies everywhere!' I stopped short, looking in wonder at the three green crosses on this street alone. 'What's with all the pharmacies? Is everybody sick?'

Tariq grinned. 'Well, you wouldn't want to be caught out with a little *bobo*, would you?'

'A *bobo*! What's that?'

'Oh, it just means a sore place, like if you hurt your finger.'

'*Un bobo*! That's hilarious!' I started laughing nervously. Bypassing a woman with a pushchair, I stumbled and ended up having to grab on to a lamp-post for balance.

'Hey, Lola,' Tariq said, casually. 'You're not, maybe, a little bit drunk, are you?'

'No! I just – I had . . . Maybe.'

If I thought Tariq would laugh it off, I was wrong. He looked horrified. I could see him mentally classifying me as a Problem Drinker. I was so embarrassed, my face was on fire.

'You should have some water, or something. Or a coffee. You don't want to be caught drinking at lunch time. On your first day.'

Now I was terrified. Caught drinking! On my first day! What was I thinking?

'Don't look so scared!' Tariq said, as we reached the

34

school. 'You'll be quite all right. Just go to the nurse's office and tell her you need to lie down for half an hour.'

'No!' I was terrified of anyone in authority finding out. Was he crazy? The nurse would sign me up to Teenage Alcoholics Anonymous before you could say *bonjour*. 'I'll be fine, honestly.' We showed our cards and went through reception together. At least, I blundered in like a dog squeezing through a cat flap, while Tariq wiped his feet, shook his umbrella with an elegant flick and folded it neatly.

Walking down the corridor with Tariq was completely different to walking by myself: a torrent of waves, greetings in different languages and high-fives. Even if I hadn't been so ill, it would have been exhausting.

'Are you all right?' he asked, looking down at me.

'I do feel a bit ropey actually.' I pressed a hand to my face.

'What do you have next? Which class?'

'Um – French.' Was it French? It was definitely something like that.

'French. With Xavier?'

'Who?'

'Monsieur Archet. He's very interactive . . . I would skip it, if I were you.'

'Everything OK here?' It was a teacher. Young and pretty. Actually she might have been a teaching assistant; I thought I'd seen her before, though all my faculties were pretty hazy right now.

Tariq beamed at her. 'Fine! Lola here is just feeling rather unwell.'

35

'Oh dear,' the teacher said. 'What's the matter?'

Tariq looked down at me. 'I think it might be that chicken you had last night, Lola – do you think? Some kind of food poisoning, anyway,' he said smoothly to the teacher. I couldn't believe what a good liar he was.

'You should probably go and see the nurse,' the teacher said.

'We tried, but we couldn't find her. D'you think you could just sign a sick slip for her first?' Tariq asked, with a charming smile. 'You just need to lie down for a while, don't you?' he added, to me.

'You know we're not really supposed to do that . . . OK, Fine.' The teacher was practically giggling at him. I don't know if it was his Grade Rep badge, or his dimples or his handsome face, but he clearly had her wrapped around his little finger. We went to the office, she scribbled a slip, and told me to go and see the nurse that afternoon.

'I'd wait till you've sobered up,' Tariq said, as soon as she was gone. He looked very disapproving.

'Good idea. Thank you! You're a great . . .' Unable to think of the word I wanted, I patted him on the shoulder. 'See you later.' And I weaved my way towards the staircase and my room.

Chapter ten

The mortification, like a bruise, took a day to really show itself.

The afternoon was fine; I just went to sleep, too befuddled to realise what had just happened. The next morning, I woke up with a mild hangover and a sick feeling about how stupid I had been. What was I *thinking*?

When I saw Vee at breakfast, I wanted to slink straight past her as I was embarrassed, but she waved me over.

'There you are! What happened to you yesterday?' she said. 'I thought maybe you went back to England. Or maybe you were dieting. You're not dieting, are you? You don't need to. And diets are evil.'

I shook my head, though it was true that I'd lost weight recently. When I started Year Twelve I was a bit chunky. But while the whole thing was happening, I wasn't able to eat properly for three weeks, and I lost just over a stone, which never came back. Obviously it was very wrong to be pleased about this and I should love myself at any size. But I was secretly pleased.

'Oh, my God, Vee,' said a voice behind me. 'Let the poor girl eat her breakfast first.'

Someone slid into the seat opposite us; the boy I'd seen yesterday wearing the leather trousers. His accent sounded English but he looked Japanese. He was very handsome, and also better at eyeliner than I was.

'Kiyoshi,' he said, holding out a hand. 'Nice to meet you.'

'Hi – I'm Lola.' My heart sank again as I remembered that my first words to everyone here were a lie.

I thought Vee might have forgotten my absence but she was like a dog with a bone.

'So where did you go?'

'Oh. I just . . .'

It was on the tip of my tongue to say, 'Actually I got drunk by myself!'

I don't know why I had that impulse. Probably I was nervous and wanted to sound funny, or rock'n'roll. But I stopped myself. *Be less Delilah*, I told myself.

'I . . . met my godmother for lunch,' I said, awkwardly. 'She was in Paris for the day. And in the evening . . . I had loads of work to do so I just powered through.'

They both nodded; obviously they were going to pretend to believe me, even if they knew that 'work' was code for 'curled in a ball crying about my bad decisions'.

'Where are you from?' said Kiyoshi.

'London!' I mumbled.

'So cool! I went there last September, for one of my mum's shows.'

'Kiyoshi's mum is a fashion designer,' said Vee. 'He's also a brilliant artist, you should see his sketches. And an expert calligrapher.'

'I'm not an expert! That takes years. I'm terrible,' said Kiyoshi.

'Kiyoshi!' Vee said. 'How many times? We need to work on your self-esteem issues!' Vee was obviously a loyal friend – tactless, but loyal.

'Thanks, mom. Vee is my Oprah,' said Kiyoshi, grinning. 'Does anyone want anything? I'm going to get some more bubbles.'

'He means sparkling water,' said Vee. 'He's obsessed, drinks it all day long.'

'I'm legitimately addicted to it,' said Kiyoshi. 'I dread the day when they find out it gives you cancer.'

I was so relieved the topic of my disappearance had been dropped. And that I hadn't tried to make a funny story about my lunchtime escapade. To get drunk with friends might have been somewhat amusing, even a bit edgy. To do it by myself was just. Plain. Weird.

My hangover improved as the day went on, but I felt worse inside. Especially when I glimpsed Tariq between classes, striding along with Priscilla, who was looking perfect as ever in a camel coat. They probably even had matching golf umbrellas.

I couldn't believe I'd let anyone see me in that state – but especially him. What if he was telling everyone? *'You know that new girl with the pink hair? I'm pretty sure she's an alcoholic.'*

I wished I could check online, but of course I wasn't on any social networks so I couldn't. Though that wouldn't stop people talking about me, of course. I'd literally been in this school for about a day, and I was already probably a hashtag.

Over and over I replayed the horrible memory, including the awful moment when I *patted him on the arm*. How could I have done something so dumb – *again*?

I thought of the sticker Mum had on the fridge: *Wherever you go, there you are*. It used to make no sense to me, but now it did. I'd changed my location, but it would take more than a random glass of wine to change my personality. I was still the same, old, stupid Delilah, who misjudged every situation and got everything wrong, always.

Chapter eleven

Back in my room after class, I started thinking about it all again.

Not about getting drunk at lunch, but about . . . the whole thing.

If *only* I had never said it.

If only I'd been able to delete it in time.

If only it hadn't been picked up by someone with two million followers.

The media consultant that Mum and Dad hired had said that was really unlucky. 'It was a perfect storm,' she said. 'The fact that it's such a topical issue, *plus* the university was in the news – it just got traction.'

'But people say worse things every day,' Dad said. 'The internet is full of trolls—'

'Yes. But Delilah used her real name.'

'And it's quite a memorable name,' said Mum sadly. 'We picked it to be unique.'

I reached for my phone, desperate to reach out to someone who would make it better. If I still had my social media accounts I would have put out a generic moan to the universe. Or if I still had my friends I would send them a message and get a virtual hug back. But I couldn't do that now. I wasn't even sure if they knew how to get in touch with me – assuming they wanted to.

Instead I looked up my new friends online. Kiyoshi's Instagram was a work of art: street fashion, cute boys and the most beautiful photos of Paris. After a few minutes of watching his calligraphy videos, I felt as if I'd had a long massage or meditation session. No wonder Vee wanted to boost his self-esteem.

Vee, on the other hand, was even more full-on online than in person. Her Twitter bio described her as 'Cat-Lover, Activist and Anarchist' and her handle was 'VeeforVagina'. Her profile picture was one crazy eye staring at the screen. There were cat gifs and art, but most of her tweets were anti-sexism, anti-capitalism, anti-war and anti-global heteronormative cisgender patriarchy. No thought went untweeted. She ate trolls for breakfast. And she had a ton of followers – way more than I used to.

Now I felt worse than ever. I admired Vee for fighting the good fight. She was like I used to be, before I got eaten alive.

In despair, I rang home.

'Delilah!' Dad said, sounding pleased to hear from me. 'So . . . Enjoying Paris?'

'Sort of.'

'School all good?'

'Yeah, it's OK. I just—'

'You must—'

'Go on,' I said, at the same time as he said, 'Sorry.'

42

This always seemed to happen to us on the phone. Long silences, and then we ended up talking at the same time. I wanted to tell him about the lunch incident – not the whole thing, but that I did something embarrassing – but it seemed too difficult. After we managed the briefest of conversations, he said, 'Listen, love, I'm afraid I'm running late – I've got to go out. I'll get your mother.'

'Hi sweetheart,' she said, finally. 'How are you? Everything OK?'

'Yes . . . I mean, no. I don't know.' That was as far as I could before I had to bite my lip to stop tears coming.

'Lola!' Mum said, sounding distraught. 'What happened?'

'I've just made a huge fool of myself at school.'

'I'm sure you didn't,' said Mum.

She said this a lot. When a friend said something mean: 'I'm sure she didn't mean it'. After an exam disaster: 'I'm sure you did better than you think.' When I had a spot: 'I'm sure no one will notice.'

I'd tried saying 'How can you be so sure?' but it got us nowhere. It was meant well. I knew that. But sometimes it felt like she was saying, 'I don't want to hear it.'

'What happened?' she asked.

'Nothing,' I said. I didn't want to tell her now. 'Nothing major. But I made an idiot of myself and now I'm probably going to have no friends here.'

'Well – why don't you just come home then?' Mum said, unexpectedly.

Completely thrown, I said, 'I never said I wanted to come home! I just said I had a bad day, that's all!'

43

'I'm sorry, darling,' Mum said. 'I didn't mean to upset you.'

'I know,' I said, sighing. It obviously wasn't going to be a good conversation, and that was that. 'It's fine. Is Len there?'

'No – he's out with friends,' said Mum.

'Out with *friends*? But it's nine o'clock on a weeknight!'

'It was a special evening – they're having a games tournament. Your dad has just gone to pick him up.'

'What? But when I was his age, I had to be home by *six*!'

'Well, you know Lenny!' said Mum. 'He's so sociable. I don't think you'd have wanted to be out till nine at his age, sweetie.'

Of course. I was a social leper while Lenny was a man about town. I wanted to scream but there was no point.

As soon as I got off the phone to Mum, I texted him, 'What's up, munchkin? Are you keeping my room clean?'

No reply. Now I was picturing him out at a casino, suave in a dinner jacket, with blondes in diamonds hanging off his arm.

Obviously it wasn't like that; more like four boys hunched over their consoles in a room that smelled of feet. But the awful thing was, Mum was right; Lenny had always had a better social life than me. Like everyone else, he was just . . . better than me.

I knew where these thoughts were heading. I knew what I was about to do, and that it would feel bad, but I couldn't stop myself. The very definition of compulsive behaviour.

Slowly, like a sleepwalker, I typed my name into Google – my real name. I read the first few articles without feeling too much – I'd read them before. But then I flipped a few pages further, and got into the comments. If I'd thought that nobody could have hated me more than I hated myself, I was wrong.

Chapter twelve

For the next three days, I managed to avoid everyone as far as possible, sneaking out to a local café for breakfast and lunch a few times. I even avoided Kiyoshi and Vee. I spent my evenings trying to get to grips with work, and watching old episodes of *Friends*.

I was halfway through 'The One with the Dentist', when there was a knock at my door. It was Fletcher.

'Hey!' she said. 'How are you doing? I've barely seen you! I was just going to go out for a walk – maybe get some hot chocolate somewhere. You haven't had hot chocolate till you've had it in Paris! Wanna come with?'

I was so lonely, I *was* tempted. But I was discovering that loneliness was a vicious circle; it made you terrible company, so you avoided people even more. I was so miserable there was no way I'd be able to hide it and keep up with her cheery chatter.

'That's really nice of you,' I said, keeping my voice steady with an effort. 'But – I've just got so much work to do. Trying to catch up, you know.'

'Oh, totally,' she said, obviously making an effort not to sound offended. 'I hear that! So much pressure. Well, some other time!'

After she left, I felt guilty about turning her down, and promised myself that I would hang out with her next time she offered.

Then I realised something. If there was gossip about me, she obviously hadn't heard it. Maybe Tariq *hadn't* said anything. But how would I know?

I got my answer later that evening when I went down to the laundry room to retrieve a mini-wash – I had managed to pack twenty pairs of knickers and only four pairs of socks. I almost ducked behind a giant dryer when I saw who was there; Tariq himself, sorting out a huge pile of shirts.

'Oh, hello again Lola,' he said, when he saw me. 'Do you know what "Do not triangle" means? And yes, I have googled it.'

'I do actually, it means don't bleach.' Mum had a list of all the laundry symbols, and their meanings, taped inside the cupboard door under the sink. I never thought I'd feel emotional about bleach, but the thought of that cupboard door made me homesick.

'Great, thanks. Any other advice? I've never actually done laundry before.' He looked delighted with himself.

'Well, first you want to separate your whites and your darks.'

'Racist,' Tariq muttered happily, sorting through his clothes. A second later, he looked up. My face must have been whiter than his whitest whites.

'Hey! It was just a stupid joke!'

'No – I know,' I said, recovering myself. I plastered a smile on my face. 'Listen,' I went on quickly. 'About the other day . . . When you met me at lunch . . .'

'Don't mention it.'

Before I could chicken out, I asked, 'You didn't tell anyone, did you?'

'Of course not!' He frowned, and I almost melted with relief. All of those days I'd been torturing myself – and he never said a thing. He could have been lying, of course, but I believed him.

'Now, where does this go?' He picked up his bottle of laundry liquid.

I helped him figure it all out, hoping that he wouldn't notice my laundry basket, which was full of unmention-ables. I managed to bung it all in quickly, while he was distracted with the machine's settings.

'So that takes – fifty minutes? Perfect, that's time for two Pomodoros. Do you use the Pomodoro method? Best study method ever.'

'No! I've never heard of it.'

'Oh, it's great. I'll send you a link. Are you on Whatsapp?' He took out his phone.

'I'm not on Whatsapp,' I said, my heart sinking as I imagined going through this conversation fifty billion more times until I died.

'Facebook? Instagram? Snapchat? Twitter?'

'I'm not on anything. I'm taking a social media break,' I said, like the big fat liar I was.

To my surprise, Tariq looked at me with admiration.

48

'That is *so* cool,' he said, raising an eyebrow. 'What a great decision. Your life must be so productive! Did you just decide to cut it all out because of the IB?'

'Um – sort of,' I said, cringing inside as I imagined what he would say, if he knew the real reason.

He looked at the time on his phone. 'Well, got to go. See you later!'

I was a bit disappointed that he'd disappeared so quickly. But honestly, what did I expect? He'd been in this school forever; he already had friends, not to mention a girlfriend. It was probably just as well. The more I got to know people here, the more risk of them finding out who I was. Monica, Rachel, Phoebe and the rest were the only safe friends for now.

Chapter thirteen

It all started so innocently. All I wanted to do was make friends.

That is – I wanted to make friends *and* impress people. Specifically, people at universities.

I had applied to loads of universities, but I had my heart set on one. I won't say what it was, but let's call it Dream Uni. Meanwhile, I was really busy; with my Junior Prefect stuff, the basketball team and Model United Nations. I didn't want to give everything up just to focus on A-Levels. I wanted to be well-rounded, so that I could put interesting things on my UCAS forms.

And part of being well-rounded was having a good social media presence. I figured that if employers looked at your social media profiles, why wouldn't universities? So along with gifs and cat videos, I posted links to interesting articles, and I retweeted and favourited interesting things. And I tweeted against things that were sexist, racist or otherwise bad. It didn't always have much effect but at least I tried. I couldn't understand my friends who just posted selfies of themselves all day long.

I also followed the universities I wanted to go to. And the Student's Union of Dream Uni. The day that Dream Uni Students' Union followed me back, I actually jumped for joy.

And then came an even more exciting day. I was fuming over a sci-fi film I'd just seen. It had only two female characters and they were both naked. I tweeted, 'Seven hundred years in the future and a woman still needs to take her clothes off to get in the story. Not cool.' And I at-mentioned the production company, and hashtagged the film. And @DreamUni *retweeted me.*

I screamed so loud that Mum actually came running.

'They retweeted me! They retweeted me!' I said, waving my phone at her.

'Is that all? I thought you'd had an offer from them or something,' she said, when I told her.

'No, but . . . it's the next best thing!' How could she not understand? If the Student's Union were retweeting me, the admissions people were bound to notice. But more importantly, it meant, surely, that I was the kind of person who belonged there. I was so proud that they'd already heard the name Delilah Hoover.

For the next few weeks, I tweeted back and forth casually with @DreamUni – not so much that I was a stalker, but just enough that they wouldn't forget me. And I also started to get interested in the other thing they were tweeting about: the Student's Union elections.

All the candidates for president looked pretty great. The two front runners were a guy called Tashfiq Raham and a girl called Liberty Bennett, who was gay. But one famously horrible newspaper columnist wrote a snarky article about British universities, trashing Dream Uni by name, and directly mentioned Tashfiq as an example of 'angry minorities'.

When I saw the link to the article on Twitter, and read it, I practically choked on my Pop-Tarts. It was so gross, I had to say something. So I drafted a tweet that said, 'Ignore this ignorant woman. I support all the candidates. #celebratediversity'.

But that was so boring! Also I didn't like that hashtag – making these students sound like they were pets in my diversity zoo. I didn't just want to write a supportive tweet, I wanted to write something that was supportive *and* witty and memorable. Something that would impress people. So I wrote, 'If the president of DUSU is not a straight white man, I'm withdrawing my application! #stuffstupidwhitepeoplesay'.

That was clunky, though. The wittiest tweets, and the ones that got the most retweets, were always the shortest. I decided to go for out-and-out sarcasm, without the hashtag. I wrote, 'Yes! Sick of minorities moaning. Straight white people FTW!'

But that looked clunky too. Maybe I should just retweet the horrible columnist and write, 'Ugh, gross'. But that was lame. Surely I could do better than that? What was wrong with me? I stared in frustration at the screen.

'Delilah,' Mum called. 'Come and have dinner.'

'Hang on,' I called back. 'I'm just writing a tweet.'

Mum put her head around the bedroom door. 'Delilah. Internet Sabbath. We agreed – remember?'

'Oh yeah.' In the interests of family unity, Mum had decided to impose a twenty-four hour 'technology Sabbath', starting at on Friday evening. We had agreed that nobody would be allowed online; not Dad, not Lenny, and especially not me. 'Hang on – I just really need to do this first.'

'Can't it wait?' Mum said.

I shook my head. This was urgent. If I didn't tweet about it now, it would be too late. And if I stayed quiet, it would look like I was condoning it. I was positive that Dream Uni – not to mention all of Twitter – would be looking to me for my reaction.

So I went with my original tweet. But at the last minute I deleted 'straight' to make it punchier and just put, 'Yes! Sick of minorities whining. Give white people a chance!'

I considered adding the hashtag #stuffstupidwhitepeoplesay, but I didn't want to overdo it. Everyone would know, from looking at my timeline, that I was being sarcastic.

'Delilah! Come on!'

'OK! Fine!' I pressed tweet and went to dinner. Five minutes later, I couldn't resist having a peek under the table. @DUSU hadn't favourited my tweet and I was a bit disappointed.

Mum saw me. 'Delilah! Stop! *This* is why we need this digital detox. Give me your phone now. Let's all put our phones away.'

She took all our devices away, and put them in a biscuit tin. And the next day we all went out for a long, healthy walk and a pub lunch where the food took ages to come. By the time we got home, and picked up the first message on the landline to tell us what was happening, the damage was done. And it could never be undone.

Chapter fourteen

It was my first Friday night at Jean Monnet. From out of my window, I could see lights, people, movement. I'd been trying to focus on my maths homework, but I kept getting distracted. I'd seen a poster earlier, that said the Film Club was showing some old film in the cafeteria. Maybe I could sneak down there and sit at the back. Like a homeless person in a library, I wanted to be in a warm room with other people.

I ran downstairs, straight into Vee and Kiyoshi who were sitting in the reception area.

'Hey – there you are!' said Vee. 'We were just saying we hadn't seen you all week.'

'I actually knocked on your door earlier, but there was no answer,' said Kiyoshi.

'Oh, did you?' I couldn't hide my grin, I was so over-whelmed with pleasure. 'Sorry, I must have had my head-phones in.'

'We're going out for some food. Come,' said Vee, thrusting her hands into the pockets of her trench coat.

'Do you like sushi?' Kiyoshi asked.

They were going out for sushi. Of course they were.
My friends sometimes went to Nandos or Pizza Express.
I had never actually been to a sushi restaurant – even if I
could manage the raw fish I was bound to impale myself
on a chopstick or try to eat the decorative green grass or
something. But if they really wanted me to come, I didn't
want to pass it up.

'I don't know if I'm dressed for it . . .' I plucked at my
hoody and jeans.

'We're not dressed up,' said Vee. She was wearing
wide denim culottes, old tennis shoes and a red blouse
plus lots of eyeliner. Her curly hair was in a big knot on
top of her head, and she was carrying a bag that said I
KNIT SO I DON'T KILL PEOPLE. 'Anyway you look
good. Your hair is so awesome. I was thinking of dyeing
it that colour but don't worry, I'm not going to copy you.'

'Here's Priya,' said Kiyoshi.

'Priya! This is Lola. She's new and she's awesome,'
said Vee.

Priya was very pretty and tiny – almost doll-sized –
with an incredibly high-pitched voice to match. She
seemed to be constantly on the move, bouncing from one
foot to another. She was also very into dancing; I had
seen her dashing to and from class, with her dance stuff
crammed into a backpack. Tonight she was wearing a
denim jacket with a colourful portrait of a woman on the
back.

'I love your jacket! Is that a Bollywood star?' I asked.

'No. It's Frida Kahlo,' she said, giving me a weird
look.

56

Oh, no. She clearly thought that I'd said that because she was Asian. I went red, completely unable to explain myself.

'She does look very Bollywood there – it's the colour scheme,' Vee said. I smiled at her gratefully.

As we left the building, she fell in step beside me. 'So how's it all going?' she asked.

'Fine . . . I'm panicking over IB stuff a bit.'

Vee shook her head. 'Don't let the hype get to you. If you look at all the great entrepreneurs, loads of them dropped out of college or didn't go.' She started typing furiously on her phone. 'Sorry,' she muttered after a second. 'It's just this idiot – I've been trying to educate him about misogyny but it is not working.' She explained the background to the Twitter row she was having with a guy about a sexist remark at an awards show.

'You agree with me, don't you?' she said.

'No, you're absolutely right,' I said, because she was. Though I was less sure when she said the guy was 'too stupid to live.'

Suddenly I had a horrible thought. Vee obviously followed every single Twitter storm going. So surely she would have seen mine? It was only six months ago. What if one of the pitchforks raised against me was hers?

Well, if it had, I had only myself to blame. I tried to snap out of my funk and listen to her.

'Anyway,' she was saying. 'I don't really care about school work. I want to study art. So all that really matters is my portfolio.'

'Where do you want to do that?'

'My dream would be to go to the Slade in London,' said Vee. 'But my parents want me to study something "sensible" like politics or economics. My plan B is computer programming but they don't even think that's a proper job.'

'What? That's crazy!'

'I know. Anyway, I really want you to tell me all about London. Do you know I haven't been since I was ten? I'm dying to go back.'

'I don't know why you would want to leave Paris. It's so beautiful,' I said.

We were on one of the streets that curved down from the Jardin du Luxembourg to Boulevard Saint Germain. The night was drawing in, but each dinky shop window illuminated a solitary sculpture or a few antique books; candles glowed from the teeny-tiny restaurants. Soft yellow lamps lit the pavements, which were wet from the recent rain. One of the navy-and-green street signs told me this was rue Monsieur le Prince. Even the names here were beautiful.

Vee gestured dismissively with her cigarette, looking very French suddenly. 'Of course I love Paris, but this area has really changed for the worse – too many rich Americans. We'll show you the real Paris,' she added, squeezing my arm suddenly.

'Thanks!' I was touched. I couldn't really understand *why* Vee was so keen on me – but I certainly wasn't going to question it. As long as she never found out who I really was, we could be great friends.

Chapter fifteen

The restaurant was very cool and minimalist, with paper screens and wooden furniture. The staff seemed to know us and there was some chit-chat in Japanese between them and Kiyoshi, as we sat down, plus bowing. I thought bowing was something racist people had made up, but obviously not. Once again I realised how little I knew about the world.

Although Priya ordered a beer, the others were having something called soba tea. They were all so mature. I ordered soba tea as well; there was no way I was risking alcohol.

I nearly spat my tea out when I realised it was cold – but luckily I stopped myself in time.

'You OK?' Kiyoshi said. 'Have some bubbles.' He poured me some of his sparkling water.

'I'm totally fine!' Once I got used to it, the tea was nice. 'I'm just wondering what to have . . .' I added, hoping none of the others would hear, 'I'm not really such a fish person.'

'No problem. They do a vegetarian set – look.'

59

I smiled at him gratefully. He was so adorably and unbelievably nice, not to mention handsome. I wondered why he didn't have a boyfriend.

'Are you a vegetarian?' Vee asked eagerly. 'Or a vegan?'

I shook my head reluctantly. That would be too much of a lie, even for me.

'I've definitely considered it,' I said, feeling guilty.

'I can send you some videos,' she said, 'that will literally make sure that you never eat meat again.'

'Or anything else,' Kiyoshi said, grinning.

When the food arrived, the others all got out out their phones to Instagram it.

'Lean in!' said Vee, motioning to all of us to huddle for a picture. There was no choice; I had to do it. I forced a smile, and watched, my hands going cold, as she casually uploaded it – where, I didn't even know. Instagram probably. Suddenly my stomach clenched.

'I'll be back in a sec,' I said. And rushed to the bathroom.

I splashed cold water on my face, locked myself in a cubicle and pressed my hands over my eyes, trying to breathe deeply. *Calm down,* I told myself. *It's just one photo. Nobody will see it.* But I knew this was just the beginning. How did I ever think I could keep my picture off the internet? Sooner or later, I'd be found out.

I walked back out to join the others, and let them all chat while I concentrated on manipulating my chopsticks without spraying sushi everywhere.

'*Oishi-desu,*' said Kiyoshi to one of the waiters, who came by to ask how everything was.

'Does that mean it's very good?' I asked him, mentally filing the expression away.

Kiyoshi smiled. 'Yes! *Oishi* means delicious. Very important word.'

Do you speak Japanese?'

'No, I just like learning languages.' Suddenly I could feel everyone's eyes on me. 'That's sort of why I'm here,' I added. 'I want to improve my French.'

They looked a bit sceptical, and I didn't blame them. Nobody needed to improve their French so urgently that they changed schools mid-way through February.

'So . . .' I said, to try and change the subject. 'Where are you all from? I mean how long have you all lived in Paris?'

'Five years,' said Vee. 'My mum is French. My dad is English. We lived in Boston until I was twelve . . . and now we live in Paris. So I'm not really from anywhere.'

'My dad is Dutch and my mum is from Kolkata,' said Priya. 'I was born in Brussels and we lived in four countries before I was fourteen. Now we're in Paris. I'm not really from anywhere either.' She shrugged.

'My parents are both Japanese but I've never lived there,' said Kiyoshi. 'I was born here in Paris, but I've always been in international schools. I guess I'm . . . Japofrench? I don't know where I'm from.'

They all looked at me.

'I'm a *bit* like that . . .' I said cautiously. 'My mum is Welsh and my dad is from Huddersfield, in the north of England. And we used to live in York. But now we live in London.'

Everyone laughed. Thank God they all thought I'd made a deliberate joke. But I'd never felt so white-bread and boring in all my life.

There was a load of gossip about people I didn't know, though Tariq's name came up when they were discussing the Student Council elections.

'He is *so* in love with himself,' said Vee. 'You know he won't let anyone take a photo of him at a party, or around people who are drinking, or doing anything unless it's getting an award or something?'

'Why not?' I asked, interested.

'Because he wants to be a politician and he doesn't want anything tarnishing his image. It's like, come on. You're running for president of a shitty student council, not the United States.'

'Tariq and Priscilla *are* like the Obama and Michelle of Jean Monnet, don't you think?' said Priya, laughing.

'They wish,' said Vee.

'Did you hear? They're both going to run for Student President,' said Priya. 'That's got to cause some upset, don't you think?'

'I'd vote for Priscilla over him,' said Priya. 'I like Tariq, but the Student Pres is always a boy . . . I'm sick of it.'

'I'm not voting for either of them,' Vee said. 'They're so entitled. And the system is corrupt. I'm spoiling my ballot.'

I almost gasped. I couldn't imagine spoiling a vote – the idea of voting was totally sacred to me, even if it was just a student election. People had died for the right to vote. No matter how bad the choices, you had to vote for the least bad option. But I wasn't going to say so.

They started talking about more people I didn't know. As I looked around the restaurant full of strangers, I felt more and more dislocated from my surroundings. What was I doing here? I wished I was in Nando's with my old friends. Or . . . with my family. What were they doing right now? Probably all at home, with a pizza. Don't cry, I told myself sternly.

Vee turned to me, while the others were talking about their Higher Maths teacher.

'I'm sorry,' she said. 'Are we being really boring?'

'No, it's fine.'

'I know it's hard at first, being new. I only came to Jean Monnet two years ago.' She made a face. 'I joined in the middle of term too. It was awful. It's like you're entering this really complex ecosystem . . . and you've got to adapt to survive. But it gets easier.'

I began to relax. 'Yeah – that is what it's like. You feel like a kind of invasive species.'

'Like a rabbit in Australia,' Vee said.

'I hope I don't get myxomatosis,' I said.

We both started laughing. And I decided that I had been worrying too much. Vee was full-on, but she was fun and interesting; plus she obviously had a big heart and was a loyal friend. Which wasn't something I could afford to pass up right now.

Chapter sixteen

After my exciting Friday evening, the weekend seemed lonely and hard to fill. I woke up on Saturday morning and looked out of my window at the courtyard below, so busy during the week, now deserted except for the three bare chestnut trees. They were just beginning to put out tiny buds. *Positive omen*, I told myself sternly.

It was also increasingly hard to stay off the internet. Even though I'd deleted all my accounts, I still missed being able to flip through Instagram, Twitter and Snapchat, on a neverending loop. My fingers were actually itching to do it – but for some reason, it seemed very important that I stay offline. Partly to protect myself, and partly to prove to Mum that I wasn't an internet-addled teen. It was so annoying the way she always said that – especially given how much time she spent on Facebook and Mumsnet.

Thinking about Mum, I wished I could be there at home, having an argument with her, right now. She wasn't answering her mobile, so I phoned the landline.

'Hi, love!' Dad said. 'So . . . first weekend in Paris! How was your Friday?'

'Yep,' I said. 'It was—'

Just at the same moment, Dad said, 'I read that—'

'No, go on,' we both said, at the same time. I told him about going out with the others. Dad told me about an article on Paris's markets that he'd been reading. I had the horrible feeling that he'd saved it, *in order to have something to say to me.*

I didn't understand where our relationship had gone wrong. When I was little, Dad used to take me swimming, and I'd ride on his shoulders around the pool pretending to be a baby octopus – classy. We even used to watch *Star Trek* together, cuddled up on the sofa. Now, we were like strangers on a train.

The sad fact was, even before the internet catastrophe, Dad and I were growing apart. He seemed to feel that now that I was a teenage girl, he should leave me to Mum, while he focused on Lenny. So that was what happened.

'Is Lenny there?' I said now.

'Yes, he is,' said Dad, sounding relieved. 'I'll get him for you.'

'Sup,' said Lenny, after a long pause. He sounded out of breath.

'Nothing – what's up with you?' I said. 'Have you just been jogging, or – no. Don't tell me. I don't want to know why you're *panting.*'

'Just been on my Segway,' Len said.

'Your *what?*'

Lenny had wanted a Segway for ages and talked about saving up for it. Obviously that was never going to happen since he didn't have a job, and since Mum and Dad considered Segways dangerous and ridiculous. Didn't they?

'Where did you get a Segway from?'

'Parents,' Len said, briefly.

'What? Since when do Mum and Dad want you to have a Segway?'

'Dunno,' he said. 'Wednesday? That's when it arrived anyway.'

He sounded like he was chewing something.

'What're you eating?' I asked. 'I can barely hear you.'

'Pain au chocolat,' he said, indistinctly.

Pain au chocolat? That was meant to be a Sunday treat!

'But it's Saturday!' I said. 'What's next? Are they going to put a Coke fountain in your room – in *my* room?'

'Course not.' Chew, chew. 'How's Paris?'

I had considered telling Lenny the truth, but now I was too annoyed. '*Mervulendo*,' I said, which was 'fantastic' in Delilish. 'The people here are really cool. We went out for sushi last night.' I didn't even know why I was saying that. I just wanted to impress him.

'Cool,' he said. 'I knew it would be fun. I'd love to go to boarding school tbh.'

'Len, I've told you before. You can't *say* tbh. You sound like a moron. You can write it, but you can't *say* it.'

'OK, Delilah,' he said soothingly. 'Relax.'

This made me even more speechless than the Segway. Was Lenny really being more mature than me? Or was he just winding me up? Either way, I got off the phone feeling even worse than before.

I tried to think positive. There were six other girls on my corridor. Surely one of them could be a friend? There was Fletcher, of course, and I would definitely try and hang out with her this weekend. Then there were twin sisters – Huan and Jiao, from China. They were friendly enough, but very quiet: they stopped talking every time I walked into the room. I would have liked to practise my Mandarin with them, but I knew they were there to learn English.

Then there were three gorgeous blonde girls. At first I thought they were all Scandinavian but now I knew Lauren was from South Africa and Mette and Kristina were Swedish. I had already seen more of them than I'd bargained for; they all had fantastic figures and strode around the communal showers butt-naked.

It seemed too early to knock on anyone's door, so I went off to have a shower. Lauren was in there, brushing her teeth.

'Are you choming cho the boarders' outing chomorrow?' she asked indistinctly, in between brushes.

'Definitely! What was it again?'

She spat, rinsed and put her brush down. 'It's a trip to the Louvre. Then Mette and I are going shopping, and for tea at Angelina's . . .' As she continued chatting about her plans for the weekend, she went to one of the cubicles, sat and peed, *without closing the door*. I was so shocked I could barely keep a normal expression on as I rinsed out my toothpaste, keeping my eyes carefully fixed on my reflection.

'Later!' Lauren said cheerily, after flushing and washing her hands.

'Later!' I said faintly. Was that a South African thing? Or just a boarding thing? Either way, it was definitely an eye-opener. I would have loved to tell Ellie about it – but of course, I couldn't.

I considered seeing what Fletcher was doing, but a note on her door told me she was away with the Athletics Club. With nothing else to do, I put on my coat and went out. I walked as far as the Pont des Arts on the Seine, which was a wooden pedestrian bridge filled with people hanging around and taking pictures. I paused for a while to gaze at everything; the Louvre, the quays with their booksellers and stalls, Notre Dame in the distance, and behind me a fabulous golden dome that I couldn't even identify.

The beauty of the city, with its spring light falling on the pale facades and dove-grey roofs, did lift my spirits. But it also felt pointless if I couldn't Instagram it or Facebook it. And it wasn't because I was a social media addict, as Mum would have said. I just wanted to share it with somebody.

Chapter seventeen

I spent the rest of the day walking – all the way from the river back up through the bustling rue de Seine with its outdoor market, to the Jardin du Luxembourg. With its blonde gravelled paths and perfectly clipped green hedges, it was a pretty cool back garden to have. Though officially, it was the garden of the Palais du Luxembourg, whatever that was – just another palace; they seemed ten a penny here.

As I walked, I started to feel a bit better. Who needed friends anyway? I liked this new self: a mysterious, aloof figure, going for solitary walks in Paris in my long overcoat, while the wind lifted my hair. Paris was certainly somewhere you could walk all day long and never get bored.

I stopped to watch a few kids in dinky cords and jackets playing with toy boats on a huge round basin. The smell of roasting chestnuts from a nearby stall made me suddenly homesick for Oxford Street in winter and Christmas shopping with Mum.

The views from the park were as spectacular as the place itself. I could see the Eiffel Tower, and a big grey dome which looked like St Paul's Cathedral, plus a huge skyscraper I couldn't identify. I noticed that everywhere there were beautiful statues of women on high pedestals, imposing among the bare trees. A sign told me that these were the Queens of France, erected by Marie de Medici in the 1600s. I squirrelled that fact away to tell someone, though I wasn't sure who would be interested.

Maybe I could try contacting Ellie at least, if not the others. But I didn't think they would want to hear from me. And they would ask where I was, and then everything would fall apart. It was easier to just leave it – to disappear into my new life.

'Hello,' said a voice beside me, in English. 'You want come and talk?'

'Um – no thanks,' I said, heart pounding. I didn't want to talk to a stranger, not to mention this guy was at least ten years older than me and looked like a murderer.

But he wasn't taking no for an answer. I had to speed up, walking faster and faster, until he finally dropped behind.

That was the second time that had happened today. The guy before had known I was English too. I wondered how high their success rate was – did anyone ever turn round and say, 'Yes, actually, I would love to hang out with you, sinister park stranger'? I didn't know if it was a cultural gap or just harassment, but either way, it wasn't nice.

If I'd had my normal resources, my instant reaction would have been to message all my friends, or even post a tweet saying what had happened. And I would have had a ton of messages in support. But now that I was offline, I had to manage my bad feelings all by myself, and I didn't like it one bit.

Chapter eighteen

When Sunday came, and it was finally time for our boarders' outing, I was practically clawing the walls.

The group waiting in the reception area was much smaller than I'd expected. The girls were all there, bar Fletcher, but hardly any of the boys had shown up. The only males to make it were Jun, a very tall and silent Chinese boy and Richard, a very small English guy with glasses and an eager expression. Even our Head of Boarders – Mr Woods, a hipstery American guy who taught English – looked like he was dreading it. Clearly the Boarders' Outing was not an A-List event.

'Hey!' Richard said to me. 'Live long and prosper!'

'What? Oh.' I looked down. Unable to decide on an outfit, I had pulled on my *Star Trek* T-shirt – a gift from my dad after his most recent Trekkie convention. I had thought it was discreet, but Richard could obviously spot a tiny Enterprise logo at twenty feet.

Like a twit, I heard myself saying, 'Live long and prosper. Or as they say in Vulcan: *Dif-tor heh smusm.*'

Richard's mouth dropped open. 'Wow,' he said. 'You speak *Vulcan*?'

'No, no.' I was already regretting this. But I didn't want to be unfriendly, so I said, 'Just that phrase. And a bit of Klingon.' In the background, behind Richard, I noticed that Tariq had arrived. Surely he would have better things to do?

'Klingon!' Richard said. 'That's even better! Say something in Klingon.'

His eyes were riveted on me. What a pity I'd never had a boy my own age look at me that way.

'Sure. Um . . .' How was this happening? '*Qastah Nuh*. It means, "What's happening."'

'Quester Nuck,' Richard repeated obediently.

Tariq was approaching us. I said, 'Great.'

'Quester – no, I've forgotten it. What is it again?'

'Qastah Nuh,' I told him, dying inside.

'She speaks Klingon!' Richard told Tariq.

I smiled weakly, wishing the ground would swallow me up. Tariq said, 'Cool!' and escaped quickly; I couldn't blame him.

Soon Mr Woods herded us into an awkward crocodile and we were off, down rue Bonaparte. On our right was the Place Saint-Sulpice, at its centre a white marble fountain guarded by four enormous stone lions. The sun sparkled on the falling water; pigeons scattered as people went by in their Sunday best. And this wasn't even one of the sights of Paris. It was just a square. Though I'd seen all this before, I would never get tired of it.

Ahead of me were the three blonde girls, their perfect bottoms swaying in denimed unison. Jiao and Huan were

73

somewhere behind me, chatting happily together. They were like the toys in Toy Story; they only came alive when you left them alone. Unlike me. Being left alone seemed to be making me even weirder.

'Hi!' said a voice beside me.

I braced myself for more Klingon lessons. But it was Tariq. I was torn between relief that he'd rescued me from being alone, admiration at his good manners, and shame that he was having to do it *again*.

'How are you?' he asked. 'What've you been up to this weekend?'

I hesitated. The truthful answer was: homework, wandering around Paris by myself, and doing a Buzzfeed quiz on which item of stationery I was. (A pencil, apparently).

'Mainly working. Oh, and I went out for sushi on Friday night with Vee and Kiyoshi and Priya,' I said, happy to show him I *had* friends – just not on me. 'How about you?'

'Usual routine,' he said. 'Fencing and study on Saturday . . .'

Fencing? I knew were were in Paris, but what was he, a Musketeer?

'Then out with Pris on Saturday night . . . We saw that film, you know the one where the White House gets blown up during the State of the Union and only the security guard survives?'

'Let me guess,' I said. 'He manages to defeat all the bad guys despite having no weapons, appropriate training or backup?'

'I'm shocked!' Tariq said. 'How did you know? You must have seen it.'

I shook my head. 'Just a guess.'

'Tariq!' It was Mr Woods. 'Can you come here a second?'

'Yes, sure!' Tariq said promptly. 'To be continued,' he added to me.

Chapter nineteen

The metro station was called Mabillon. I was learning that each station had its own character; this one seemed the epicentre of studenty, hip, bustling Paris, always surrounded by teens in skinny jeans and big scarves talking and smoking simultaneously without drawing breath. With its Art Nouveau sign and green-and-white tiles, it was prettier than any underground transport system had a right to be. Maybe that was why everybody here was so beautiful and well dressed, I mused. Living among such beauty, all day every day, some of it had to rub off.

Down on the platform, Tariq was talking to Richard and Mr Woods, so I forced myself to go up to the Three Blondes. They welcomed me in a friendly enough way.

'Photo op!' said Kristina. As they leaned in for a selfie, I was almost blinded by all their teeth.

'Come on, Lola!' Mette told me, as they went for a second one.

'No, it's fine!' I said, shrinking away from the camera again. 'I look awful today,' I added in explanation.

'No, you look great!' said Lauren, shaking back her gleaming blonde hair. I wondered if she ever had a moment's self-doubt or even a spot or a bad hair day.

'So, do you have a boyfriend?' Kristina asked me, as we rode the swaying train.

When I shook my head, she said, 'How long have you been single?'

Seventeen years? I thought. The truth was, I had never really had a proper boyfriend. The closest I'd ever come was five confusing weeks with Dane Willet, whose underwear was always showing *and* who dumped me on my birthday.

'A while,' I muttered.

'You'll definitely meet someone in Paris,' said Mette. 'Everybody does. I lost my virginity the week after I got here!'

'I waited a month,' said Kristina. 'But I didn't start *enjoying* it till I met Fabrice. He's so much better than Stefan was.'

My jaw was on the floor. They were talking in totally normal voices, like they were discussing homework. And Mr Woods was only a few people away, down the carriage. He could hear them and they didn't care!

It was official: these were not my people. They were all perfectly nice – but they were terrifying in their extreme lack of self-consciousness. Forget my dodgy past; if they knew I'd been here a week without losing my virginity, I was fairly sure they would disown me.

Eventually we emerged from the train at rue de Rivoli, and crossed the road to go through an arch in a high wall.

77

Once again my jaw dropped, but this time it was from all the splendour around me. The Louvre seemed to stretch as far as the eye could see: a set of imposing facades, gathered around the glass pyramid that was flanked by fountains. Beyond the courtyard where we stood was a huge park, unrolling far into the distance.

'Ok, folks, huddle!' said Mr Woods.

We herded together, joining all the other tour groups milling around.

'I know most of you have already been here. You've already seen the Kim Kardashian of the sixteenth century, AKA . . .'

'The *Mona Lisa*!' said Richard.

'Right! But, guys, the Louvre wasn't always an art museum. It was built in the 1200s and soon became one of the palaces of the kings of France. It was François I, in the sixteenth century, who decided to mix it up. He tore down all the old medieval stuff and pimped this crib into the Renaissance pad we see today . . .'

I cringed inside. Mr Woods was nice, but he was obviously one of those teachers who thought we couldn't understand anything unless it was framed in slightly out-of-date pop culture references.

'Then in the 1680s it was pause, record scratch, and the royal court was relocated to where?'

'Louis XIV moved it to the Château de Versailles,' said Jun in his quiet voice. Jun was in my History class and it was clear that he knew far more about European history than any of us. In fact, I had yet to hear him answer a question wrong in any class.

'Right! He was sick of living in town, and he wanted to be able to kick back with his nobles and make a place that would be ... the Coachella of the seventeenth century.'

Turning away, I caught Tariq's eye. He was obviously trying not to smile, too.

'And that was where I think he made his worst mistake,' said Mr Woods. 'Because moving the court to Versailles meant that the nobles lost touch with what ordinary people were thinking, which led 100 years later to ... Any idea?'

'The French Revolution,' Lauren said.

'Of course, the French Revolution. And during the Revolution they obviously looted all the paintings owned by the royal family and the nobles. Kind of like they did during the London riots, isn't that right, Lola? And they decided to put them here, for ordinary people to enjoy them. Like us! So in we go.'

I found myself beside Tariq in the queue. He said quietly, 'So in the London riots, did they focus on seventeenth century oil paintings – or were they more into the eighteenth century?'

'It was mainly sculpture,' I said, with a grin.

Tariq laughed. 'He is really a great teacher,' he said. 'He just ...'

'Doesn't trust us to understand anything earlier than Jay-Z?' I suggested.

'The way he put it is that school is analogue and we need to make things digital,' Tariq said.

I groaned.

Inside, the marble floors echoed to the noise of thousands of visitors, their feet squeaking beneath the serene stares of Greek and Roman marble statues. Our bags were checked very thoroughly and we all had to walk through metal detectors, before we were finally allowed in.

We went straight to the room with the *Mona Lisa* in it. Mr Woods didn't have to tell us this; it was obvious from the enormous crowd gathered around one of the pictures. The others all surged forward to take pictures of it over the heads of the crowd – all except Jun, who started carefully examining one of the other paintings. Jiao and Huan were taking pictures of each other methodically in front of every painting in the room.

'You don't want a selfie with the Kim Kardashian of her day?' Tariq asked me.

I shook my head. 'I hate it when people do that – just take a picture of a thing without even looking at it.'

'They don't need to look at it. They just need proof they were here.'

We moved away to look at the other paintings in the room. One of them showed a man who looked like the *Mona Lisa* except with longer hair, pointing upwards at the sky.

'Hey guys,' said Mr Woods, joining us. 'Pretty rad, huh? This is *John the Baptist*, also by Leonardo.'

Once he dropped the pop culture references, his explanation of the painting was actually very interesting. The group reconfigured and we went on and on, past endless masterpieces. The names began to blur together; Raphael,

Leonardo, David, Delacroix . . . I could feel myself getting distracted. Tariq was with the blonde girls, who were giggling over some nudes. Mr Woods was explaining a painting to Jun and Hiao.

'Think of self-portraits as the selfies of their day,' I heard him say.

'Lola!' It was Richard again. 'Don't you think this one looks like Captain Kirk?'

'A little bit,' I said, looking sideways at the portrait.

'Which is your favourite episode?'

I tried to come up with a few for him, inwardly deciding that I would never wear that T-shirt in public again. Why had I ever admitted I knew anything about *Star Trek*? I knew why, of course. I couldn't resist showing off – even something as pathetic as my knowledge of Klingon. From now on, I would try and *think* before I spoke.

Chapter twenty

After we finished in the Louvre, we went outside and walked through the Jardin des Tuileries: another beautifully manicured expanse of gravelled paths, stone fountains and green hedges. It felt as if we should have been sweeping through it in crinolines and powdered wigs, instead of Nike trainers and North Face backpacks. At the end of the garden, a Ferris wheel turned slowly. Beyond it, way in the distance, was the Arc de Triomphe. It lined up so exactly with the arches in the Louvre that it was like looking through the wrong end of a telescope.

It was warmer and sunnier now, and everyone was taking off their coats. We were heading towards a green-roofed little pavilion where the plan was to get hot chocolates. Beyond it I could see what looked like another museum.

'That's the Orangerie museum,' Mette told me. 'And across the river – the big building that looks like a railway station – that's the Musée d'Orsay. Great place to meet guys!'

I was starting to realise how much there was to see in Paris, and how little I had seen of any of it. If I stayed here for years and years, I wouldn't even touch the surface of it.

'Isn't it great?' said a voice beside us. 'I always feel like I should be in a periwig and silk trousers when I'm here.'

It was Tariq again.

'Yes, I was just thinking that!' I shook my head. 'It's so beautiful though . . . it's almost overwhelming.'

'I know,' Tariq said. 'Sometimes, when I've been here for too long, I get sensory overload. I just feel like I need to see some concrete or barbed wire or something to let my brain rest.'

I laughed; Mette looked puzzled.

'Luckily my parents live in Dubai, which is extremely restful, because there's a bit less to do there,' Tariq said.

'Is that where you're from?' I said. I didn't think so, but I didn't want to assume either way.

'No.' He sounded very empathic about it. 'I'm from Lahore. In Pakistan.'

'I know where Lahore is,' I muttered. Then I kicked myself. He was probably always having to explain where it was. 'Are there good museums there?'

'Why, yes, there are. Actually we have the oldest museum in Pakistan. It's very famous – though the Louvre is a *slightly* bigger deal.' He grinned.

Mette, obviously bored, drifted off to join the others. I tried to think of something else to say.

'So,' said Tariq, 'Are you doing Klingon as your language option?'

I went horribly red again. 'No! It's my dad, he's really into *Star Trek*. So I've picked up bits here and there.' *Why did I keep on talking about my dad and Star Trek?*

'Have you got brothers or sisters?'

'One brother. He's thirteen going on fourteen.' I added, 'My parents just bought him a Segway.'

'A Segway? Gosh. I got a new bike when my sister went to boarding school. Now I feel short-changed.'

'Really?' I stopped short. 'Is that a thing?'

'I don't know if it's an actual, official thing. But it definitely happens. It's like they feel sorry for the one who won't have the joy of wearing pants with their name sewn into them for eight weeks at a time.'

I laughed, though, like a loon, I felt myself blushing at the mention of pants.

'I am lucky that I'm boarding in Paris, though,' he said. 'My sisters all boarded in England for their secondary school. But I wasn't keen on that, for various reasons. Not least, the boarding schools are all in the middle of the country. There's nowhere to get your hair cut, or buy clothes, so you end up looking like a homeless person.'

I thought he must have led a sheltered life if he thought boarding-school kids looked anything like homeless people. He looked immaculate as ever, even though he was dressed down today – with jeans, a black woollen coat, and a navy scarf looped around his neck. Even his white Van trainers looked clean. I considered saying, 'Damn, Tariq, at it again with the white Vans,' but I decided we'd had enough out-of-date pop culture for the day.

'So how many sisters do you have?' I asked.

'Three. One lives in Dubai with my parents, one's at Cambridge, and one lives in Islamabad.'

'So . . . If your parents live in Dubai, and Pakistan is home, how did you end up in Paris?' I asked curiously.

He laughed 'It does sound shady, doesn't it – like they were trying to get rid of me. Basically, we lived in Lahore until I was twelve. Then we moved to Paris, and I enrolled here at Jean Monnet. My dad got a job in Dubai, last summer – he's a diplomat. I didn't want to move again, especially since there was the option to board – so I stayed here.'

'Oh, I see. That must have been hard?'

Ahead of us, Jun was leaning in for a picture beside a grinning Mette.

'A little. But . . . Jun came here at the start of the year, by himself, to learn English and French. He'd didn't know anyone here at all; he'd never been away from China before. So that puts it in perspective.'

'Oh. I suppose.' I felt a little embarrassed. Now *I* was the one who sounded sheltered.

'I don't think I'd want to live in Dubai anyway,' he said. 'I want to go back to Pakistan again. But first I've got my five-year plan.'

'You have a five-year plan.'

'Sure. First, do the IB. Then, study history and politics – probably in the UK, but I'm also applying to the States. Then after that, I wouldn't mind doing a political internship. Ideally I'd gather enough experience so that I could be really useful when I went back to Pakistan.' He shrugged. 'That's the current plan, anyway. In five years' time I'll make another plan.'

I nodded and tried to look as if I had my life under equal control.

'You think it sounds too much?' he said. 'Priscilla says I'm like Stalin with my five-year plans.'

Hm. This was the second mention of his girlfriend today. If he was making a point of it, there was really no need. He was cute enough, with his green eyes and his glossy black hair that kept flopping over his forehead. But he was far too smooth for me, even if he hadn't had a girlfriend. Nonetheless, I did think he was a nice guy. I couldn't understand what Vee had against him – or Priscilla.

'Maybe we should join the others,' I said, and we turned towards the pavilion. Two kids, a brother and sister, ran past us shrieking. I felt a surge of envy at Lenny again, but not for the Segway. Because he got to be at home.

'So have you joined any clubs or anything?' Tariq asked.

'None really. I'm so busy catching up with the IB stuff.' That must be why Tariq kept talking to me; he couldn't get enough of my sparkling repartee. If there was a Boring Club, I could probably join that.

'Why don't you get involved in the Student Council?'

I hadn't been expecting that. The obvious answer was 'Because I'm a fugitive and I don't want to draw attention to myself,' but I didn't say that.

'I know that the Entertainments Committee could do with someone to publicise the Spring Ball.'

'Their what?'

'The Spring Ball.' He grinned. 'It's only the biggest thing to happen in Jean Monnet since the . . .'

'Winter Ball?' I hazarded.

'Exactly! That's just the kind of quick thinking they need. It's at the end of May. The fact that you haven't heard of it tells me they need more help with publicity.'

Publicity! Posters, flyers, maybe a web page. Meetings, committees, decisions, oh my! I *was* tempted.

But they would want me to go online. I'd have to have my photos in the yearbook. Or I'd end up on a web page . . . In any case I would be drawing attention to myself, which I didn't want to do.

'Fletcher is the Entertainment Officer,' Tariq said. 'She's doing a great job, but I'm seeing the whites of her eyes a lot these days. If you did change your mind, I'm sure she'd love the help . . . No pressure though.'

Damn. He was a good politician – giving me the same charming, lop-sided smile that he had given that teacher in order to get the sick slip from her. This was obviously the whole reason he'd wanted to talk to me – to inveigle me into helping.

But it sounded like such a nice idea. I couldn't hide away forever. I would have to start living my life at some point. And this time I would be more careful.

Don't give into impulse again, Delilah, I warned myself. But something told me this would be a good impulse.

'OK!' I said. 'I'll do it.'

Chapter twenty-one

On Monday morning, we had assembly in the main hall – known here as a 'community meeting'. Unlike the room in my school, which doubled as the gymnasium and always smelled faintly of deodorant, this was a big, vaulted space with an enormous painting of someone carrying an enormous cross up the steps of a building. Who that was, I had no idea, obviously.

I got there early, hoping to catch Vee or Kiyoshi in a way that wasn't too obvious. But they weren't there yet. I saw Fletcher arrive, late and out of breath, with her boyfriend Hunter in tow. I'd noticed her earlier from my window, trotting across the courtyard in her running gear while I was barely awake. I turned round before she could spot me. I had decided who I wanted to be friends with; getting involved with other people would only confuse everyone.

In order not to look conspicuous, I killed the time by examining the student artwork hung at one end. My eye was caught by two or three drawings of landscapes – ruined tower blocks overgrown by trees and flowers. I leaned in and saw Kiyoshi's name. He was so talented – was there anything he couldn't do?

'Yo,' said Vee, behind me. 'How's it going? How was your weekend?'

She was wearing a tattered tweed overcoat with several badges on it. One of them said 'Ni putes, ni soumises' which I didn't understand; the other said 'Kill the Bankers' which was clear enough.

'It was good! I went to the Louvre. . . .' I decided not to mention agreeing to get involved in the Entertainment Committee. 'I got to know some of the other boarders. It was fun.'

'Oh, good. I was worried that you might have been lonely during the weekend. Kiyoshi and I went for crepes on Sunday. We would have messaged you but you're not on Snapchat or anything . . .'

I nodded, feeling sad at how I'd missed out. It was true that she had my phone number, but that was way too formal – like a written invitation. 'How was your weekend?'

Her face darkened. 'Don't ask.'

I could tell she *did* want me to ask, so I was going to when we were interrupted by everyone being called to sit down. The director of the school went up to the podium. He was a short, powerfully built Belgian guy called Monsieur Mougel, and apparently he'd been in the UN peacekeeping force before becoming a teacher. He didn't look as if he *wouldn't* make us do drills or dawn marches.

'Welcome everyone. As you know, this week is International Autism Awareness Week.'

I didn't know, and I wasn't sure what to expect. But it was interesting; we watched several videos about autism, and heard from one of the maths teachers whose son was autistic.

'Now we're going to hear from someone in our community who's going to talk about his own experiences. Please welcome Felipe.'

I was amazed to see a tanned, skinny boy from one of the years below make his way up to the platform. With his huge glasses, and his trousers belted way too high up on his waist, he looked incredibly vulnerable. He went up the stairs so slowly and reluctantly, my heart was in my mouth for him. Vee and I exchanged anxious glances.

When he got to the podium, he could barely look up. When he finally did, his face froze into an expression of horror as he took in the size of the crowd before him. There were a few moments before he could speak, and when he did it wasn't what I'd expected.

'Shit!' he said.

Everyone burst out laughing – but not in a mean way; you could feel the goodwill. The whole room clapped and cheered, which made the boy smile uncertainly. After a few quiet words with one of the teachers, he started to speak again.

'Hi,' he said, reading from a piece of paper. 'My name is Felipe. I have autism. This means that I find some things difficult that other people find easy.'

In his quiet voice, Felipe went on to talk about how he found loud noises and crowds overwhelming, how he got anxious when his routine was disrupted, and how difficult he found it to make eye contact. He was obviously painfully nervous, but you could feel the entire assembly willing him to make it through to the end – which he did.

'So if I avoid your eyes,' he concluded, reading from his sheet, 'It doesn't mean I don't want you to talk to me, because actually I do. Thank you.'

As he hurried back down the steps, the whole room erupted in applause. Beside me Vee was clapping and cheering Felipe. I felt very strange suddenly.

'That was amazing,' I said in a shaky voice. 'But won't it just get him bullied?'

Vee looked at me in surprise. 'Of course not. We don't really have bullying here. It's because we share our stories. We're honest.'

I nodded, feeling more ashamed. The idea of being honest was obviously so foreign to me, I didn't even recognise it when it stood up and talked at assembly.

The meeting ended with an announcement from Tariq and Priscilla, about a collection of old clothing for charity. They were obviously quite a practised double-act.

'We'll accept anything clean that's still in good condition,' Priscilla said.

'*Even* if it's from last season,' Tariq quipped, to general groans. Vee was right – he *did* look a bit smug.

As we all filed out, Richard, my Trekkie friend, gave me a wave. 'Live long and prosper!' he said, holding up his hand in a Vulcan salute.

'Live long and prosper,' I muttered, blushing as I saw Tariq approach.

'Still on for Wednesday?' he asked.

'Yes – see you then!' I said, knowing that I was going pink.

'What's happening on Wednesday?' said Kiyoshi in my ear. 'Hot makeout sesh with Tariq?'

'No,' I said. 'Just a, um, class thing.'

I was paranoid that Vee would ask me more questions, but she was too deep in her own misery.

'It's my parents,' she said, when we asked.

'What have they done now?' said Kiyoshi.

'They don't want me doing Art. At all. They've spoken to the school – without asking me – and I'm doing Economics instead.' Vee looked close to tears.

'Can you get one of the teachers to talk to them?'

'No.' For a second I thought she was going to cry, but she was made of sterner stuff than that. She blinked a few times and said through gritted teeth, 'I'll just have to work on my portfolio in my own time.'

'And in the summer,' said Kiyoshi, soothingly. 'You'll have time. I'll help you.'

'I'm really sorry, though,' I said. 'It's horrible that they won't support you.'

'Thanks.' She sighed, and scuffed the floor with her worn Nike. Suddenly she looked up. 'What did Tariq want?'

'Oh, nothing – it's just a thing for, um . . . History class,' I improvised. I felt bad for lying. But I wanted to keep it on the down-low for now. For one thing, the committee might not even want me, in which case the others wouldn't even have to know. And if I *did* end up on the committee . . . I would just cross that bridge when I came to it.

Chapter twenty-two

It was nice to have a class that I liked on Monday morning. I walked into Greek and Roman literature feeling a bit less alien than I had the week before. Mr Gerardo was wearing a particularly spiffy dark blue floral shirt and braces. I lived in hope of seeing him crack out a bow tie.

'I trust we all had a pleasant weekend,' he said, 'and that you're all ready to be plunged into some nice eighth-century warfare? Good. Can you turn to Book One, line 200?'

After we had read a few pages, Mr Gerardo said, 'This fight between Achilles and Agamemnon. Why does Agamemnon refuse to return the slave girl to her father?'

'Because . . .' I *knew* this. This was Iliad 101. I just felt flustered. 'Um . . .'

'Isn't it because of pride?' said someone at the back.

'Yes, it is. And why is his pride involved?'

Priscilla frowned. 'Well, Agamemnon sees this girl as his property. So if he gives her up – he's losing face.'

'Yes!' Mr Gerardo said. 'And another way of saying that is what? What emotion will he be feeling?'

This one was easy.

'Shame,' I said.

The feeling of so many faces turning round to look at me, once so familiar, was suddenly terrifying. I looked down again at my printout, remembering why I had vowed not to talk in class.

Mr Gerardo nodded. 'Shame – fear of being shamed before society – is *the* driving force of the *Iliad*. If you think of it, the reason they all want Helen back isn't because of any particular concern for her, but because of the shame of having her taken. Agamemnon refuses to give up his slave – because of the shame that would entail. So Achilles refuses to fight, again to avoid dishonour. And then, after Patroclus is killed . . .'

There was a gasp from someone in the back of the room. Everyone laughed. 'Oh dear – I should have given a spoiler alert,' said Mr Gerardo. 'Anyway, Patroclus is killed, I'm afraid. And the shame of having caused his friend's death is what drives Achilles back out to the battlefield to face Hector. Achilles knows that Hector will kill him – the goddess Thetis has told him so – but the shame of not doing it would be worse than death. In a sense, pride, honour and shame are what drives all the figures in this epic. Yes, Priscilla?'

'They're all just acting like a group of schoolboys,' she said crisply.

Mr Gerardo laughed. 'Yes, that's certainly one side of it,' he said. 'It's true that they could have sat down and worked it all out reasonably. But that would have made less of a story. And in any case, aren't we all a mixture – with heroic qualities and less heroic ones?'

Nobody said anything.

'It's true that our standards are different now,' he went on. 'We don't have such an emphasis on shame any more, in our society. What do we have instead?' He sprang over to the whiteboard, and wrote Shame –> Guilt. 'We have guilt. And this is a transition that you see in Greek literature. The *Iliad* deals with shame but by the time we come to read about the Peloponnesian war and Herodotus, we'll have moved away from that towards guilt instead. Instead of having their behaviour dictated to them by society, Greeks will listen to their conscience to decide right and wrong.'

He paused. 'Can anyone tell me the difference between shame and guilt?'

I certainly wasn't going to say anything. Priscilla said slowly, 'Is it that guilt is something you feel inside – and shame is something other people put on you?'

'Yes. Exactly. Another way of saying that is that guilt is private, and shame is always public. Let's go on with this passage.'

I felt my pounding heart settle a bit as the class went on. But I kept thinking about what Mr Gerardo had said – that we didn't have shame any more in our society. I couldn't help thinking he was wrong about that.

Chapter twenty-three

I had done so well with staying off social media. I had stopped even wanting to passively scroll through all the gifs and selfies of friends-of-friends. But the uneasy feeling from my Greek and Roman class stayed with me, until on Wednesday afternoon, I cracked. I found myself going online and looking up my old friends. Nisha had posted a picture that said, 'When all your friends come out with you on a Tuesday to celebrate your birthday!' They were all in it, all smiling at the camera. Jules had changed her hair.

Of course I *knew* that Instagram only showed part of the picture. I *knew* it didn't mean that they were having a great life all the time. But it wasn't a complete lie either. They *had* had a good night out. Without me.

And they all looked better than I did. I really didn't look great; the roots on my new hair were showing and my eyebrows were out of control. Why had I ever called myself Lola? Lola was the name of a minx. As opposed to a . . . a hamster like me.

'Hey! Lola!' said a voice. It was Fletcher.

'Oh, hi!' I said, flustered. I closed my laptop before she could see what I was doing.

'I just came to get you, for the Entertainment Committee meeting!'

'Oh yeah, of course.' I looked at my watch. A quarter to five; how had I nearly missed that?

'I feel so bad that I'm not doing all this!' Fletcher said breathlessly, as we hurried down the corridor. 'Are you sure you can manage it on top of all your school work?'

'Well, of course. I mean we have the same amount of work, don't we? You probably have more than me, since I'm doing the certificate.' I still hated admitting this.

'I guess! I just always feel I should be doing more.' She laughed, but there was a sort of hysterical edge in her voice that made me think that if anything she should be doing *less*.

The Treasurer was a plump Swiss-American guy called Patrick, who had round glasses and an air of quiet amusement. I'd seen him hanging around with Tariq. Then there was an English girl called Rose, who was Social Secretary. She had a very fruity, posh accent and a regal way of talking very slowly while staring into the distance six inches in front of her.

'This is Lola,' said Fletcher. 'She's offered to help us with publicity, isn't that super awesome?'

Rose didn't seem to think it was awesome, but she accepted my presence with a nod.

'As long as Tariq and Priscilla agree . . . Where are they?' she asked.

'I didn't see Priscilla in school today,' said Patrick. 'She might be ill. Good to have you on board, Lola!'

I beamed at him. As I took out my special designated notebook, I felt like I was home again. I remembered how excited I used to feel, sweeping down the corridors at school with my prefect's badge. I felt like a real mover and shaker, and whenever we got to sit in on a staff meeting, I felt like I was in the West Wing. This wasn't the same, but it was close.

Except that I had forgotten my pen. Not a great omen.

'It's OK!' said Fletcher. 'I have tons. Here.' She passed me an expensive-looking rollerball pen.

'Let's start without them,' Rose was saying. 'So. I've drawn up a list, and one thing we should definitely have is a mani-cam.'

'What is that? Is it some kind of surveillance unit?' said Patrick.

'No, no,' said Rose. 'It's a way of filming peoples' manicures. They have it at the Oscars. You get a cardboard box, put a little bit of red carpet inside it, and then you film people's fingers "walking" inside it. So it's like the mani is walking the carpet.'

We all looked at her doubtfully.

'Also,' Rose continued. 'What about a VIP area?'

'A what now?' said Patrick – except in his Swiss accent, 'What' came out as 'Vot.' He pushed his glasses back up his nose.

'We wouldn't call it that obviously,' said Rose. 'But I think, since we're doing all the organising, it's only fair that we should have an area where we can relax and hang out with our friends and our dates.'

'Um, maybe we should wait for Priscilla before discussing any of this?' Fletcher said tentatively. 'And Tariq,' she added.

'Well . . . let's not decide anything, but we can put together a list of suggestions,' said Patrick. 'What have you got, Fletcher?'

Fletcher got out a thick notebook with a very impressive set of colour-coded sections. 'Since we're allowed to serve wine and beer, we should really serve food as well so that people don't get drunk. I was thinking mini-pizzas and crisps?'

'Hm,' said Rose eloquently.

'What do you mean, hm?' said Patrick.

'No, that sounds *so* lovely, but it doesn't really go with the theme, does it?' said Rose.

'What is the theme?' I asked.

'It's a Venetian masked ball,' said Rose. 'So obviously we can't serve mini-pizzas.'

'Well . . .' I closed my mouth. I was way too new to point out that pizza seemed appropriate, if it was Italian.

'Pizza seems appropriate, if it's Italian,' said Patrick.

Tariq came in at that point. 'I'm so sorry I'm late, guys,' he said, pulling off his scarf.

'Where's Pris?' said Fletcher.

'I have no idea,' said Tariq. 'I haven't heard from her all day, which is weird. What have I missed?'

'We've mainly been discussing manicures. And snacks,' said Patrick, looking long-suffering.

'Ah,' said Tariq. 'Good. I like snacks.'

'But it's a *masked ball*. How can people even eat when they have their masks on?' Rose burst out. 'And who's going to want to eat while they're wearing couture?'

Now Fletcher looked panicked. 'I didn't know people were wearing couture,' she said. 'My dress is from Zara.'

'I love Zara,' I said, to stick up for Fletcher. 'What's it like?'

'Guys,' Patrick said, pained. 'Can we stay on topic?'

Just then, Mr Gerardo appeared. I was surprised to see him, before I remembered that he was our Pastoral Head of Year.

'I would not normally interrupt you all in your inner sanctum,' he said, sitting down. 'But I want to talk to you about the ball.'

'It's cancelled?' breathed Fletcher.

'No, no,' said Mr Gerardo. 'But we are concerned about the theme.'

'What's wrong with the theme?' said Rose, looking indignant.

'We just think it's placing too much pressure on students to come up with an expensive dress or suit, *and* a mask. After the Winter Ball, we realised that students were spending far too much on their outfits and it was causing stress. We've had quite a few emails from parents also. We think the spending is getting out of hand.'

'But – the masks are only a hundred euros or so,' said Rose. 'A good one, at least. You can get crappy ones for much less.'

'That's still rather a lot of money,' said Mr Gerardo. 'I think there was a linguistic misunderstanding, too. The Student Council described it in their original email as a *bal costumé*. And that doesn't mean masked ball. It means fancy dress.'

'Fancy dress?' said Rose, in tones of disgust. 'You mean, like, dressing up in as clowns?'

'Not necessarily,' said Mr Gerardo calmly. 'You can come up with creative ideas. We just don't want anyone buying anything new – it has to be something you already have, or that you can make.'

There was a stunned pause.

'That's really not going to be popular,' Tariq said reluctantly. 'A lot of people have bought their outfits already.'

'They can wear them for the Graduation Ball,' Mr Gerardo said. 'Let's have a show of hands. All those in favour of changing the theme from masked ball to fancy dress?'

Fletcher raised her hand. So did Mr Gerardo. Rose folded her arms. After a glance at her, Patrick kept his hand down too. I felt deeply relieved that I didn't have to get involved in this.

Mr Gerardo looked at me. 'I don't think I get a vote,' I said quickly. 'I'm not actually on the committee.'

'All right,' said Mr Gerardo. 'Tariq?'

Tariq raised his hand slowly, looking torn.

'Great. Then it's decided, three to two. The theme changes to fancy dress.'

Rose sighed loudly and stabbed her notebook with her pink fluffy pen.

'What kind of fancy dress, though?' Fletcher asked. 'We still need a theme.'

'World War Two?' suggested Patrick.

'Where you all dress up as Nazis? Perhaps not,' said Mr Gerardo.

'I know!' said Rose. 'How about a Chinese theme?'

'How do you mean?' said Mr Gerardo.

'You know – we could have our hair up with chopsticks, like those . . . what are they called . . .' Rose indicated her own glossy dark hair. 'Geishas!'

'Geishas are Japanese,' said Tariq.

Rose waved a hand. 'Well, we could make it Asian-themed.'

There was a shiver in the room and we all instinctively turned to look at Mr Gerardo.

'That's not such a good idea,' he said. 'Ethnicity isn't a theme.'

'No, but if they're minorities . . .'

'Hmm,' Mr Gerardo said. 'It depends on how you look at it. If you and I went to China, wouldn't we be minorities there?'

'I suppose,' said Rose, clearly having her mind blown by the very idea. Now it was my turn to look down. *I* had used the word 'minorities'.

My heart was beating crazily now and my palms felt clammy. This was reminding me too much of – things. I should never, ever have become involved in student politics.

'Any other suggestions?' said Mr Gerardo.

There was an awkward silence while we all looked at each other. My mind had gone blank.

'I have one,' Fletcher said suddenly. 'How about a party where we all come as the meaning of our name?'

'How do you mean?' said Tariq.

'Well, everyone's name has a meaning. So mine means someone who makes arrows, so I could come with a bow and arrow . . .' she trailed off uncertainly. 'I mean, not a real bow and arrow. Obviously.'

'That's a brilliant idea!' I said excitedly. 'Patrick, yours means a nobleman – from the Latin – so you could come in a suit with a monocle, or something.'

'What does mine mean?' said Rose.

I caught Tariq's eye. 'Um – I think it just means a rose, doesn't it?'

'So I could come as a rose?' she said, perking up.

'I like that,' said Mr Gerardo. 'What does everyone else think? Show of hands?'

Everyone's hand went up. I felt weak with relief.

'I'll leave you to it,' said Mr Gerardo. 'Good work, Fletcher. And Lola – impressive etymology skills.'

He smiled at us and I felt the glow of once again, briefly, being a good student. What would I wear? Delilah meant 'delight' or 'temptress.' Which had all kinds of possibilities, if I was brave enough to explore them.

'What does Lola mean?' Fletcher asked.

I jumped in fright as I realised how close I'd come to forgetting I was Lola.

'Oh,' I frowned. 'I – I'm not sure. No, wait, I think it's from Dolores which means "sorrow".' Phew.

'You could wear a little black dress – it could be really cute,' said Fletcher.

'Ooh yes!' said Rose. 'Or a long black dress. That would look great with your hair actually.'

'Guys,' said Patrick again. 'Can we please?'

The rest of the meeting went smoothly. With Rose distracted by looking up rose costumes on her phone, we managed to agree on pizzas and, instead of a mani-cam, a cheap Polaroid camera. Fletcher said she would do the social media aspect if I could take charge of making and distributing posters and flyers.

'Here – thanks,' I said as we were leaving, giving her back her pen.

'No, no, you keep it,' she said.

'But – it looks expensive . . .'

'Keep it! Have it! I have tons of them!' she said.

There was clearly no point in arguing. I walked out of the meeting feeling taller and happier than I had since I'd arrived. It was so nice to be on a committee again. But even nicer was being able to spend time with people, without having to try and make them my friends.

'Great work there, Lola. How did you know what Patrick meant?' Tariq said, catching me up.

'We had a book of baby names in the house and I used to spend hours poring over it.' I managed not to add that said book lived in the loo; that was a visual he could do without. 'And for Rose . . . I just took a guess.'

He laughed. 'She's a nice girl – she's just not super bright,' he said. He lowered his voice. 'I was there when she discovered water polo *wasn't* played with ponies.'

I laughed.

'Are you busy on Friday night?' he said.

'I'm not sure,' I said automatically. There was no chance that I'd admit, 'Probably not.'

'The Film Club is showing *Ridicule*. It's a great film – set in the court of Louis XVI. One of my favourite Louises. Hm. What do you think the plural of Louis is?'

'It can't be Louises ... Probably just Louiiiis?' I pondered this.

'Anyway. You should come. We're all going. Me, Priscilla, Patrick, Nicolas – have you met my friend Nicolas?'

'Yes – sure, sounds good,' I said, trying to conceal my excitement. It looked like I had made another friend. At least – Lola had. I had a feeling that Tariq wouldn't have much time for Delilah at all.

Chapter twenty-four

By Friday, I was feeling *so* much better than I had on Monday morning. I decided to give home a quick Skype call after class, just so they knew that I wasn't permanently miserable.

'I'm so pleased, darling!' Mum said, when I told her about joining the Entertainment Committee. 'That's brilliant! You could even think about running for the Student Council now, couldn't you?'

I rubbed my forehead. This was typically overoptimistic of Mum. 'I've only been at this school about five minutes.'

'Listen, have a word with your brother. He's about to go out.' She yelled, 'Len!'

'Sup,' he said, a minute later. I blinked. He looked *older*. Still no stubble but he definitely looked *bigger*. And was it my imagination or did his voice sound deeper?

'Sup to you too,' I said. 'Where are you off to? Hot date?'

After a minute he said, 'Actually, yeah.'

I could not believe this. Lenny had a *date*? My baby brother, who would say 'Yuk' whenever he saw a kiss on screen, and was scared of sharks in the swimming pool, and made us stop the car to catch a Jigglypuff – out on a *date*? Had the world gone mad?

'Who with?' I managed to say.

'Holly,' he said. 'You don't know her. She's in my year group.'

Holly! I tried to picture this ship – Len and Holly – but I couldn't. 'Where are you even going?'

'Starbucks. She has to be home by seven-thirty because her auntie's coming over and her mum's making a paella.'

I was honestly too bewildered even to tease him about it. Plus – there was the sad fact that Lenny was going on an actual date, while I was further than ever from having a boyfriend. He was totally growing up, and he didn't need me for any of it.

'Well, have fun!' I said, heartily. 'Stay safe!'

It was a stupid thing to say, but to be fair, I was in shock. Lenny was becoming a proper teenager, with a girl-friend whose mum made paella. Where would it all end?

'So,' Mum said, reappearing. 'Did Len tell you about his date?'

'Yes!' I said. 'I can't believe it! Have you met her?'

'No, but I've seen pictures,' said Mum. 'She looks about twenty-five and has better make-up than I do.' She laughed.

'But what is she like? Is she a good influence?'

'She's fine, Delilah. Perfectly nice kid. Talk to your Dad.'

I nodded, bracing myself for another awkward encounter.

'So – what's this – you've joined a committee?' Dad said, poking his head round. 'That sounds more like the Delilah I know.'

I smiled. He sounded more relaxed than usual – more like the dad I used to know. 'Yeah . . . it's just planning a party, but still. I think it'll be fun.'

I explained the theme to him, and as I'd suspected, he was disappointed that I wasn't going as Uhura.

'Dad, I can't go as Uhura,' I said. 'For one thing, I think a blackface costume would not be a tactical move.'

'How are you going to do Delilah though?' said Dad. 'I hope you're not . . .' He was obviously having nightmares of me in a temptress-style bra top and harem pants.

'Don't worry, Dad,' I said, soothingly. 'I'm going as Lola – remember? Dolores. Sorrow.'

'You're going as Lola?' he said, clearly as stunned as I'd been by Lenny's date.

Mum reappeared. 'You're going as Lola?' she repeated.

'Well – yeah,' I said patiently. 'That's kind of the whole point of me being here, right?'

'I know, but—' They both stared at me.

Mum said, 'Love – Delilah – you know that this whole escape thing won't last forever, don't you? I mean there's uni to think of, the whole rest of your life . . . You'll have to go back to Delilah eventually.'

I said nothing. It was impossible to picture 'the rest of my life'. But I could easily picture the hell that my life would become, here at Jean Monet, if I was unmasked.

'Can we talk about this another time?' I said. 'I just want to stay Lola – for now.'

Mum and Dad exchanged their trademark worried glances again. 'Sure, love,' Mum said. 'Just be careful.'

Chapter twenty-five

'Hey,' said Kiyoshi on Friday at lunch time. 'Did you hear about Priscilla?'

Vee and I looked up from our baguettes. We were sitting on a bench in the Jardin du Luxembourg, across the road from the school. It was another sunny day, and Vee was still upset about her parents so, to cheer her up, Kiyoshi had declared a prison break. We had bought sandwiches in the Marché de l'Odéon – a beautiful, bustling place where you could buy about three hundred different cheeses, olive oils and antique books – and brought them to the park.

The Luxembourg Garden was already one of my favourite places in Paris – especially now, with the sun getting warmer every day, and tiny green leaves beginning to appear everywhere. Kids were being led around on little Shetland ponies; old men were playing chess under the bare chestnut trees. I could only imagine how beautiful it would be in summer. Why was the weather always nicest just in time for exams?

'What about Priscilla?' Vee said. 'Has she got a job at the UN? Leading an army perhaps?'

'No, silly. Her dad's got a new job somewhere, I'm not sure where. The Middle East maybe.'

'Oh, no,' I said. 'Poor Tariq.'

'What do you mean, poor Tariq?' said Vee. 'He'll just find another adoring girlfriend.'

'I don't know about that,' said Kiyoshi thoughtfully.

'What do you mean?' we both said, but Kiyoshi refused to say anything else.

'I wonder who else will run for Student President now,' said Vee.

'I bet Hunter will run. You know, Fletcher's boyfriend,' Kiyoshi said, carefully pushing a piece of tomato back into his baguette. He ate as neatly as he did everything else. While Vee and I were a mess of crumbs, he was as pristine as ever.

'How do you know all this?' I asked curiously.

'Kiyoshi always knows all the gossip,' Vee said. 'Everybody loves him and confides in him. He's like the opposite of me.'

Kiyoshi laughed but didn't contradict her.

'That's so weird, that Priscilla's just left,' I said. 'In the middle of term. In the middle of the week, even. It's like she's disappeared.' Not that I was one to talk.

'It happens in a school like ours,' Kiyoshi said. 'Jobs change. Parents move.'

'They'll just find another clone to replace her,' Vee said. 'The Council will continue.' She started doing robot arms and a robot voice. 'Nothing . . . Will stop . . . Their march to power.'

We all giggled, but my baguette was now sticking in

my throat. I still hadn't told them that I was on the Entertainment Committee. It was official now. I was on the email list and everything. There was also a Facebook group, but I had managed to get out of that – for now.

'Why do you hate them so much?' I asked, trying to sound casual.

'Who's them?'

'You know. The Student Council.'

'I don't *hate* them', said Vee. I just think they're mindless automatons, sleepwalking into the exact same six-figure-paying jobs their parents had, ready to ruin the world in the exact same way. They're the very definition of the one per cent.' She balled her sandwich wrapper up into a ball.

Oh, God. How could I possibly tell them now?

'Did you hear they changed the theme of the ball?' Kiyoshi said. 'It's not a Venetian ball any more. Which is such a pity. I had my opera cloak all ready.'

'What's the theme now?' I asked, feeling like a weasel.

'Come as your name,' Kiyoshi said.

'What? That's the weirdest thing I've ever heard of,' said Vee. 'What does that even mean? Do I come as Queen Victoria?'

'You could come as Victory . . . like, in a Greek toga with laurel leaves?' I suggested.

'Huh. I know,' she said. 'I'll come as the Triumph of Capitalism. With pictures of children being trampled by Coke cans and tanks and things.' She started rolling a cigarette.

'That'll get the party started,' Kiyoshi said. 'Ugh. What will I wear, though? Kiyoshi means pure.' He sighed. 'That won't be hard. I am the poster boy of pure.'

'Do you . . .' I paused. Kiyoshi seemed very open in one way, but we hadn't discussed crushes yet. 'Is there anyone you do like? In school?'

He shrugged.

'Come on, Yosh,' Vee said. 'You can tell her. He likes Marco Agnelli.'

'Shut up!' said Kiyoshi, suddenly sounding much younger. A second later, he said more quietly, 'Maybe. But he would never be interested in me.'

'Oh, I know Marco,' I said. 'He's in my Greek and Roman Lit class. How do you know he wouldn't be into you?'

'I just do. Can we change the subject? Vee, what about you? We can't *all* be tragic single spinsters. If you had to shag someone in Jean Monnet who would it be?'

Vee said, 'Nobody. Maybe if I met an older man – or woman. But why would I want some tedious adolescent to drip over me all day, like a three-legged race?'

We both nodded. Once again, I wished I was like Vee.

'My little brother has just gone out on a date,' I said suddenly. 'It's so weird. He's only fourteen. I'm worried about him.'

'It must be nice to have siblings,' said Vee. 'I bet you feel like less of a failed science experiment.'

Kiyoshi said, 'I feel more like our cat. She's a ragdoll,' he added, to me. 'They're beautiful but too stupid to go outside, so we've built her all these ladders and platforms to replicate the outdoors. It's like she's living in the

114

Matrix. Which is basically how my parents want me to live my life. They're, like, Give him the blue pill.'

I groaned sympathetically, relieved that the conversation had moved on from the committee.

The alarm on Kiyoshi's phone started ringing. 'Come on. We better get back.'

As we walked back to school, I felt absolutely sick. Vee was so pathologically honest. I couldn't imagine her lying about anything, ever. She was full disclosure, all the time. She was bound to find out about the committee some time. And then, if she found out about the other thing . . .

'Guys,' I said suddenly. I stopped dead.

They both turned round.

'I feel really stupid but . . . I have something to tell you.' I clasped a hand to my forehead.

'You're pregnant with Monsieur Mougel's baby!' said Vee.

'You're not a student!' said Kiyoshi. 'You're here undercover, like in *21 Jump Street*.'

Quickly and miserably, I said, 'I joined the Entertainment Committee. I'm helping organise the ball.'

'*What?* Why?' said Vee.

'I don't know! They needed help . . . I'm new here, I wanted to meet people.'

'It's OK, Lola,' Kiyoshi said. 'You haven't joined the Nazis.'

I could see Vee was about to say 'Nearly' but she closed her mouth. 'I just don't know why you didn't *say* anything.'

'I was embarrassed! And you obviously think they're awful . . .'

'Look,' said Vee. 'You've got to do what you want to do! Be yourself. Just be honest with us. And promise me you're not going to turn into one of *them*.'

'I will,' I said, feeling weak with relief. Though I also couldn't help thinking that those three promises might turn out to be mutually exclusive.

Chapter twenty-six

On Saturday afternoon Fletcher knocked on my door to see if I wanted to come shopping for supplies for the ball. I was pleased to be able to accept one of her invites, for once.

'Bring an umbrella, though,' she said. 'It's raining cats and dogs.'

I smiled as I found my umbrella. Fletcher was full of homely expressions like that – she had told me the other day she was at 'sixes and sevens.'

'Hello ladies,' said a voice, as we came through reception.

It was Tariq, back from fencing practice.

'Want to come with?' Fletcher said, after explaining our errand.

He looked a bit subdued, but he agreed. He was also uncharacteristically dressed-down in a grey hoody and old red cords.

We took the Metro to a department store called Bon Marché, at Sèvres-Babylone. It was as lovely as everything else in Paris – an original art deco building, with a vaulted glass ceiling, and graceful escalators that soared above a display of artificial cherry trees. Fletcher had wanted to go to a cheap shop in the Fourteenth Arrondissement, but Tariq insisted that we should buy quality equipment that we could leave to the school as our legacy.

'I'm sorry to hear about Priscilla leaving,' I said tentatively, while Fletcher was deep in the back of the shop, comparing different fairy lights.

'Thanks,' he said. 'It's . . . Yeah. It's hard.' He lifted his shoulders. 'But it's not that long until the Easter holidays. We'll meet up then, somehow.'

Fletcher joined us. 'What do you guys think?' she asked, seriously, holding up some lights. 'White, blue or multicoloured?'

'White,' Tariq and I said in unison, and laughed at each other.

'If you're finished, let's have a hot chocolate,' said Tariq.

Over hot chocolate for me and Tariq, tea for Fletcher and macaroons for all of us, Tariq started to perk up. The spring rain battered against the high windows as Tariq told us about Priscilla's new life in New York, in an apartment that overlooked Central Park. Her school was 'challenging in a good way', she'd already been invited to a party, and her parents were talking about getting a dog.

Fletcher looked wistful. 'I'm really going to miss her in track club,' she said. 'We were going to do a 10k together, it sucks that she'll miss it. And that I have to train without her. I'm glad she has somewhere nice to run though.'

'She definitely does,' said Tariq. 'And, apparently there's a place near her that does hot chocolate with edible cups. Which makes me want to visit her even more, if that's possible.'

'Aww,' said Fletcher, while I wondered if anyone would miss me when I left Jean Monnet.

'I guess, looking on the bright side . . . it's a good thing that you and Pris don't have to run against each other for Student President?' Fletcher said tentatively.

Tariq made a face. 'Yeah – I suppose so.'

'Do you know who'll run instead?' I said.

'No idea. I hope *someone* does.'

'Wouldn't you like to run unopposed?' I asked.

'No! This isn't North Korea. I suppose it depends on who gets made Grade Rep.'

'Is that just appointed by the teachers?' I couldn't hide my fascination with the intricacies of student politics.

'Normally it's a vote. But if someone has to leave in the middle of term, the teachers just pick someone,' Tariq said.

'I bet it'll be Lauren,' said Fletcher. 'Her grades are awesome and she's so nice. Or Rose maybe. The Grade Reps are always a girl and a boy,' she added, to me.

'That's a good idea,' I said.

'Yes, isn't it?' said Tariq. 'There was a big fuss when that rule was made initially – it was a few years ago.

People said it was tokenism and that people would take the girls less seriously.'

'But now everyone's totally used to it,' said Fletcher.

'I actually think the Student Pres candidates should always include at least one girl, too,' Tariq said. 'Otherwise it's always two boys running against each other. Pris and I were going to be the first to break the pattern in ages.' He looked subdued again.

'You should run, Lola!' Fletcher said to me. I laughed out loud.

'You have to be in the school longer than two years, or I'd agree,' Tariq said, smiling. 'Why don't you run, Fletcher?'

'Me?' She put down her teacup, looking genuinely shocked. 'No way! Are you kidding? I could never.'

'Of course you could,' said Tariq. 'Why on earth not? But hey, I won't push you into it. Maybe I want to turn Jean Monnet into my own private dictatorship.' He helped himself to another macaroon. 'Tuesday would be renamed Tariqday and we'd have crepes every morning for breakfast. Also a big statue of me in the courtyard. Gold.'

We were all giggling now. 'Is that your fifth macaroon?' I asked.

'My sixth.' He brushed crumbs off his lap. 'Shopping uses almost as many calories as kick-boxing, did you know? I made that up,' he added, to Fletcher's protests. 'But that reminds me, I could do with some new socks.'

'I've had two, *and* a madeleine! I'm such a disgusting pig. But I did run a six-miler this morning,' she said to me, almost anxiously.

'Listen, I'm on my third,' I told her. 'And I'm not a runner.'

Fletcher was sweet – but every time I spent time with her, something happened to confirm that we were from different planets and would never be BFFs.

Chapter twenty-seven

On Monday, the IB One class was asked to stay behind for a special announcement after community meeting, in order to hear who was going to be the new Grade Rep. I was sitting beside Kiyoshi and Vee who was thumbing away furiously at her phone, in total breach of the school rules.

'Have you got a new game?' I asked her.

'No,' said Vee. 'I am talking to an idiot on Facebook who doesn't know the difference between a Muslim and a terrorist.'

I sighed inwardly, as I remembered happier times when I used to do that – riding my keyboard horse into battle and taking down all comers. But now . . . there was no way I could do that. Not just because I wanted to stay hidden; I just didn't feel that sure of myself or my opinions anymore.

'Your new Grade Rep is someone who works hard at her studies, and is always friendly and open to newcomers – especially within the boarding community,' M. Mougel was saying. I noticed Lauren, beside me, straightening up. She was open to newcomers all right – when it came to toilet doors anyway.

'That person is Fletcher Harrison,' he continued.

I turned round to see the shock and delight on Fletcher's face. 'Oh my God!' she said, clasping her hands to her face. Her boyfriend, Hunter, hugged her, though he looked more surprised than happy, I thought. Tariq leaned over and gave Fletcher a big thumbs-up. I was happy for her too, though I did worry that this new duty would tip her right over the edge.

'Did you see Hunter's face?' Kiyoshi said, as we went out. 'He did *not* look pleased. Maybe he wanted Grade Rep.'

'He couldn't have. The Grade Reps are always a boy and a girl,' I said automatically.

Vee gave me a funny look. 'Big deal. It's not like they've got the nuclear codes,' she said.

I laughed, and we all started making our way out of the room. With the prohibition on phones lifted between assembly and class, everyone started checking their screens – except me.

I had a text message, though. Lenny had sent me a photo.

'Hope you like my accent wall.'

'Oh my God!' I said out loud.

It was a picture of my room. One of the walls – the one furthest from the door – was painted black. And not even very well painted; I could see that the ceiling had splodges on it – and so did my bookshelf.

'I am going to kill him,' I said.

'Who?' Vee looked over my shoulder. I showed her the picture, and she said, 'It looks pretty cool actually.'

I just shook my head. I was willing to bet he'd asked them while they were deep in a box set, and they'd said yes without listening, just to get rid of him. And now I was imagining him turning my room into a love-nest for him and Holly to hang out in. Satin sheets and . . . whatever else people had. I shuddered.

'I'd love to paint my walls black but I would never be allowed,' Vee said.

As we all filed out towards the exit, Fletcher caught my eye. 'Still on for the meeting?' she said, pointing both index fingers at me. 'Five p.m., Room 18.'

'Yes – see you then!' I said, knowing that I was going pink.

'What's that about?' said Vee.

'Oh, nothing. We're just finalising the poster for the Spring Ball.'

'Of course. The Entertainments Committee. Awesome.' Vee pointed both her index fingers at me, copying Fletcher.

'Very funny,' I said, giving her a shove.

'I just don't want you going over to the dark side,' said Vee.

I laughed uneasily. Even though I had been honest with the other two, I felt as if I was cheating on them in some weird way by being on the committee. Even though that made no sense. I would have to do something about it. I was already living a double life; a triple one was too much, even for me.

Chapter twenty-eight

It was still only March, but the weather had turned freak-ishly warm. People were beginning to sit outside during breaks, turning their sun-deprived winter faces upwards. I was looking out of the window during Greek and Roman Literature, when I noticed that the chestnut trees in the courtyard had definite green buds, and there were daffodils growing underneath them.

With Priscilla gone, there were only four of us in the class – Tariq's friend Patrick, Mette and my Vulcan friend Richard. Which made for a nice atmosphere. I was loving the *Iliad,* and speaking up a lot more than I did in my other classes.

'Now, I'd like to start by reading out this passage in Greek,' Mr Gerardo said. 'You do need to hear it in Greek, I think. You'll see the translation side by side. Listen.'

I'd never heard someone read aloud in ancient Greek. I listened, absolutely rapt, as the harsh and alien syllables unfolded, totally incongruous coming from Mr Gerardo. It sounded like a language from outer space, but at the same time I kept hearing words that sounded familiar.

I started poring over the passage, and the English. Luckily, Mr Gerardo had provided a transliteration, so the alphabet would be relatively easy to crack. I underlined the vowels and began to teach myself the symbols. That meant e; that meant PS; that was a 'th' sound . . . It would be easier to learn it properly, of course, but this felt fun in a *Da Vinci Code* way . . .

'What do you think, Lola?' Mr Gerardo said.

I looked up, heart pounding. 'I'm sorry?'

Mr Gerardo's mouth twitched, and I had a feeling he knew I hadn't been listening.

'Never mind,' he said. 'Patrick?'

After class, he asked me to stay behind.

'I see you were enjoying the original,' he said, nodding at my page. 'Either that or you were doing some amateur cryptography.'

'I was just trying to decipher the alphabet.'

'Let's see.' He picked up my printout and smiled. 'Very nice and methodical. I do have a guide to the alphabet. Unless you'd prefer to crack the code yourself?'

I laughed. 'No, that's OK.'

'I noticed that you haven't joined our Facebook group yet.'

'I'm not on Facebook. Sorry. I'm not on any social media,' I added out of habit, to stop the inevitable questions. Though Mr Gerardo was hardly going to follow me on Instagram.

He looked at me curiously, but all he said was, 'Ah. Like Achilles, you've withdrawn from battle. Well, that will leave you some extra time for the IB. And maybe even for my Baby Greek class? I realise that sounds odd,' he added. 'It just means Greek for beginners. We've had some new joiners this term, so you won't be alone. Eight-thirty on Thursdays, in Room 32 on the first floor.'

'Wow! I would love that!' But then my face fell. 'It's just that, I'm having so much trouble keeping up with the IB as it is. Even though I'm only doing the certificate.'

'What are your other subjects?'

When I told him, he said, 'You sound like quite the linguist. Do you know what you'd like to study at university?'

I shook my head. I used to think History and Politics, with the idea of being a politician of some kind. But that was out of the question now. I would probably have to work in a morgue or somewhere like that, where they weren't choosy.

'You could study linguistics,' he suggested.

'Really?' This was a new idea. 'What kind of job would that get me, though?'

'That's a sad way to look at it.'

'I know, I know.' I blushed. 'Learning is important for its own sake, and everything.'

'It's vital for its own sake,' he said. 'Once you've learned something, nobody can take it away from you. In any case,' he said, sliding off the desk where he'd been sitting. 'There's no pressure regarding Baby Greek. But if you do enjoy it … It's worth paying careful attention to your enthusiasms. They help you find your happiness, I think.'

'Thanks,' I said, standing up too. 'Is enthusiasm a Greek word?'

'Yes! From enthous: possessed by a God. Which is a fine way to be,' he said. He held the door open for me as we left. 'Though my wife would say otherwise, based on the size of my record collection.'

I did a double take. For some reason, I had totally assumed he was gay. And I never would have pictured him collecting original vinyl. Was there no end to the ways in which people could surprise you?

Chapter twenty-nine

The warm weather held all week, and it was still gloriously sunny on Friday, when I met the others on the Pont des Arts. This was the wooden bridge over the Seine that connected the Left Bank to the Louvre. I thought we would be meeting there to go somewhere else, but it turned out that the bridge was a destination in itself. People had gathered for picnics, playing guitars and sipping plastic cups of wine. It was getting a little chilly, but nobody wanted to let go of the summer feeling.

'Want some wine?' Priya said. We hadn't seen much of her lately, because she had a new boyfriend. He was a posh English boy called Tyger, who was on the football team and wore a man bun.

The others were drinking red wine; Kiyoshi had his usual sparkling water. They also had baguettes, fresh ham and delicious-looking cheese. I took a plastic cup, marvelling again at how teenagers could openly sit around drinking wine here. Looking around at the view I realised I could now name some more of these magnificent buildings. That golden dome opposite us was the Académie

Française; up the river, the other golden building was the Assemblée Nationale. I hadn't been inside either of them yet, but at least I knew what they were; baby steps.

'So what've you been up to lately, Lola?' Kiyoshi asked.

'Not much. Just studying. I might be taking up Baby Greek.'

'What the hell is Baby Greek?' said Kiyoshi. 'Is that what Greek babies talk?'

Laughing, I explained, and the conversation moved on to our weekends. I decided not to mention the shopping expedition with Tariq and Fletcher.

As if she was reading my mind, Priya said, 'I heard you're on the Entertainment Committee, Lola. How's that going?'

'Oh, it's going fine . . .' I said, wondering if I had LIAR on my forehead.

'Do you have a title yet?' Vee said. 'Like, Officer, or Secretary-General?'

'No,' I said uncomfortably. 'I'm just helping out.'

'Do you salute each other?' she said slyly. 'I bet you do. Or you march around saying "Action that!"'

I laughed uneasily. To take the focus off myself, I told them about the 'Come as your name' debacle, and how the theme ended up being changed.

'It was really awful,' I added. 'We were discussing the possible themes and Rose suggested a Chinese theme. With . . . geishas.'

I felt a bit bad for throwing Rose under that bus, but the other two just rolled their eyes and laughed. Vee, though, looked furious.

'Are you going to report her?' she said.

'For what – being racist?' I said uneasily. 'Well, no. I mean, it was never going to happen. Mr Gerardo dealt with it and explained to her why it was a bad idea.'

'There you go. She's here to learn stuff, Vee,' Kiyoshi said. 'Isn't that what we go to school for?'

'Rose just isn't very bright,' Priya said. 'She once wrote a History essay where she said the Afghan war was fought with Kardashian rifles.'

'But still,' said Vee. 'She has no business being on the committee if she thinks that's OK.'

I shivered inside. Vee could so easily be talking about me.

'Vee. Priya and I are the token Asians here, so we get to decide, and we think it's not the end of the world. Honestly, I've heard so much worse. Right?' Kiyoshi said to Priya, who shrugged.

'I genuinely don't care what Rose Fitzwhatever says. I'd better go though,' she said. 'I have dance class. Don't ask me why I still do it. Ballerinas are all insane.' She unfolded herself gracefully and put on her leather jacket.

'I'd better go too actually,' said Kiyoshi. 'I have sooo much chemistry homework it isn't even funny. I'll see you guys tomorrow.'

After they left, Vee fell silent. I wasn't sure whether she was still brooding over Rose, or thinking about something else entirely. I was about to ask her if there was anything wrong, when she turned to me.

'Lola. Is there anything you want to tell me?' she said.

My heart jumped into my throat, and stayed beating there.

'What do you mean?' I asked.

'It's just that I googled you.'

I went hot and cold. 'Oh?' I said, as calmly as I could.

'Yup. And you're not anywhere. No mention of you. There are a couple of Lola Maxwells, but they're not you. It's like you don't exist.'

There was a long, long, awful pause. So obvious. How did I ever think I would get away with this?

'Well, I've been trying to stay offline,' I said. My throat was dry. I took a sip of wine.

'Is Lola even your real name?'

'Yes,' I blurted out. 'I mean, sort of. It's a nickname. Look, Vee, I *would* like to tell you.' *Another lie.* 'I just can't tell you yet.'

'But don't you trust me?' she said. 'I thought we were friends.' She looked more upset than angry.

'I do! I do trust you . . .'

'It's just, what with this, and the committee . . .'

'But I told you about the committee!'

Vee said solemnly, 'I can't be friends with someone who doesn't tell me the truth. I don't think anyone could.'

I nodded miserably. As we started packing up the picnic things, I thought: she was right about that, at least.

Chapter thirty

I was meant to be doing maths homework, but instead I was pacing around my room like a rat in a trap.

What if it was starting again?

I didn't think I could survive it a second time.

Suddenly I wasn't in Paris any more. I was back in my room at home, the evening it happened, looking at my Twitter feed.

Normally I was thrilled to see a notification, but not this time. I had thousands of notifications, hundreds of new followers, and none of them were saying anything good. I scrabbled around until I found the original tweet that was being retweeted around the world.

In a panic, I deleted it. Then I wrote 'That tweet was meant to be ironic! I was joking!' But it came out as 'That tweek was meant to be ironic'. The first reply I saw said, 'She's a racist AND she can't spell.'

That was one of the nicer comments. I skimmed over the rest, hardly daring to look, but I caught some: *Should be burned. Should be kicked out of her school. Not a human being.*

That last one caught me off guard. Not a human being? Did they really think I was *not a human being*?

I ran out of the room, almost knocking down Lenny who was practising a handstand in the hall.

'Mum!' I yelled. 'I don't know what to do. Everyone's – it's all—'

I couldn't even get the words out. Mum and Dad came and looked at my laptop.

Dad swore under his breath. 'She's trending on Twitter,' he said, glancing at Mum.

'I'm sure it's not properly trending,' I said, my voice shaking. 'I'm sure it's just trending among people I follow—' Not that that would be better, but I was clutching at straws.

Dad leaned forward to see, and said nothing.

'It's – I'm trending globally?' I said.

At that moment the phone rang – the landline. We all jumped and looked at each other.

'Isn't anyone going to answer that?' said Lenny, putting his head around the door.

'Lenny, go to your room!' Mum barked. Looking amazed, he shuffled off, and the phone stopped ringing. Mum got up to unplug it.

'I've disabled your account,' said Dad after a minute. 'So . . . it should all go away, I hope.'

But it didn't.

I can't actually remember much about the next few days, or weeks. I managed one day at school, then I came home and refused to go again. My friends all texted me, or so I was told – Mum and Dad had taken away my phone. I didn't reply; I couldn't. After a few days they stopped texting.

School was out of the question. I could barely eat or sleep; it was all I could do to stay alive. The GP prescribed beta blockers. I saw a counsellor. I stayed off the internet.

At least, I was supposed to. But it turned out that not knowing was the worst thing of all. One morning, around five a.m., I woke up after a few hours' doze, unable to bear it any more. I had to see what was happening, whether it had died down, whether there was anything new.

I went to Lenny's room, woke him up and begged him to lend me his phone – his first ever smart phone.

'Don't tell Mum and Dad,' he said blearily, handing it over.

It was like going down a whirlpool full of filthy, rubbish-strewn water. Almost the worst things were the people who *agreed* with me. Some terrifying figures were coming out of the woodwork, saying the most disgusting racist things, all in support of me – all anonymous of course. Lots of them could barely spell, but lots could, and sounded highly educated, which was almost scarier; they sounded like the kind of people I might even know. But strangely the comment I remember most, that hurt me most of all, was short. It just said SHES UGLY.

Chapter thirty-one

'Is everything OK between you and Vee?' Kiyoshi said.

I looked up at him, panicked. We were in a corner of the library, where he had offered to help me with my maths. I was already distracted after a long text exchange with Mum about my poor destroyed bedroom. Apparently Lenny did *not* have permission from Mum to paint the wall black, but Dad had agreed to it without paying attention – typical.

'How do you mean?' I said nervously.

'I don't know. It just seems there's some weirdness between you. Is it about the committee?'

'No! It's . . . it's hard to explain,' I said, doodling on my pad.

Kiyoshi sighed. 'The thing you have to remember about Vee,' he said, 'is that she was basically raised by wolves.'

I actually laughed at this. 'Literally wolves?'

'No, not literally wolves – her parents are just terrible people.'

'How so?'

'In every way. They're really, really rich and they pay her no attention at all except to yell at her. The first time I went to her house her mother barely said hello to me, just started chewing her out for leaving her window open in the rain. But not like, Hey, that was dumb. She shouted at her for five minutes straight. While I was standing there. It was so embarrassing and awkward, I can't tell you.'

'Oh.' I thought about my mum, who never scolded me in front of other people. Once they were gone, yes, but never in front of them.

'And they're just horrible people, basically. I stayed for dinner and all her mother could talk about was how lucky Vee was to be getting such a good education, and how much she could have achieved in her career if she didn't have a kid.'

'Seriously?' I gulped. 'Yikes. What about her dad?'

'Oh, he played on his iPad the whole time. At the table. While her mum got drunk. It was a horror show. I've never been back – I have to make up excuses.' He started to grin. 'Don't tell anyone this, obviously. But in my head, I call her mum Cruella.'

I started to laugh.

'Anyway, Vee is having a really hard time with them right now. Which might explain why she's being weird. I know she seems confident, but she's very insecure. I mean she's the most loyal friend in the world, but if she thinks people don't like her any more, she tends to panic and lash out at them.'

'But I do like her! It's just that she wants me to tell her something. And I can't.'

'Oh, I see,' he said. 'Well, that could be it as well. She's so open, she hates it when other people aren't. I think her parents have kept a lot of secrets from her and she's still really angry at them about that.'

Great. This was just sounding better and better.

'Kiyoshi, you don't hate me for being on the committee, do you? I mean, you don't think I'm – selling out or something?'

He laughed. 'Of course not! I don't think they're monsters, either. And nor does Vee, no matter what she says. I like Tariq, for instance. Although . . .'

'What?'

Kiyoshi looked stricken, and refused to say anything at first. Then he said, 'I'm pretty sure that he's gay. And it's a pity that he won't come out – especially if he's running for Student President. It's annoying, really.'

'But he can't be! He's going out with Priscilla, long-distance.'

Kiyoshi raised an eyebrow. 'A long-distance girlfriend is basically an imaginary girlfriend. AKA a gay boy's best friend.'

'But what makes you think he's gay?'

'It's just a feeling I get from him – the way he acts, the way he looks at boys sometimes. Little things. He always seems like he has a lot to prove. And it doesn't seem like he misses Priscilla all that much. Not that I was ever convinced by them as a couple.'

'That's such a pity,' I said. 'For him, I mean.'

Kiyoshi looked worried. 'You won't tell anyone, will you?' he said. 'I shouldn't have said anything. It's a terrible thing to out someone. Definitely don't tell Vee, she's so indiscreet.'

'But she wouldn't tell anyone, would she?'

'Not intentionally, but she can't help it – it would be all over Twitter by lunchtime. Promise you won't tell her?'

'Of course,' I said, my heart plummeting even further. Just what I needed; another secret to keep.

Chapter thirty-two

After I had said goodbye to Kiyoshi, I realised what I had to do.

I had to find Vee, and tell her the truth. I had no idea what she would say, but anything was better than living in suspense. As I paced around the school looking for her, I actually began to feel relieved at the idea of having things out in the open. Whatever she said to me, it couldn't be worse than what people had said already.

I found her in her usual spot in the courtyard, having a loud discussion with Priya, under the sign that said THIS IS A QUIET STUDY AREA.

'I'm not rich! It's my parents who are rich!' she was saying.

I went up to them.

'Sorry to interrupt. Can I talk to you, Vee?' I said. 'Like – outside? Alone? Can we go for a walk? Just up to the Panthéon, maybe?'

'OK.' She put her shoes on reluctantly. Now that the weather was getting better she took her shoes off every chance she got. She referred to them as 'foot prisons' and said her feet needed to be free.

Soon we were walking up the rue Soufflot, which led from the Jardin du Luxembourg up towards the Panthéon. I loved the rue Soufflot. It was just a normal Parisian street, not especially beautiful, but the atmosphere always made me imagine old Paris, of the years of Sartre and de Beauvoir. The cafés there were always full of school kids and university students from the nearby Grandes Écoles – the most prestigious universities in France, where Vee was doomed to go. There was also a tempting-looking creperie, which I had noticed on my lonely weekend walks, though I'd never had the nerve to go in alone. After my last debacle, I had gone off solo dining.

But the main thing that struck the eye was the Panthéon, which loomed at the end of it: a huge, imposing grey dome that looked like something out of the *Da Vinci Code*. I had assumed it was some kind of church, but in fact it was full of the tombs of famous dead French people, including Victor Hugo. I almost wished I was in there with him.

We walked mostly in silence, until we got to the Panthéon and sat down on the steps. Tourists brushed by us on their way inside, while I tried to think of what to say. The sun had gone in, and the wind blew to remind us that it was still March.

'So . . . you know how you were saying, you couldn't find me online,' I said.

'Yeah.'

141

I swallowed. There would be no going back after this. 'You were right. Lola isn't my real name. I had to change my name. Because of something that happened.' This was even harder than I'd thought. 'I was – being harassed online . . .'

'Wait!' said Vee. 'Was it something like GamerGate?'

I was about to say no, but then I looked at her face. She looked horrified *but* sympathetic. If I told her the truth, the sympathy would disappear. She would be every bit as angry as everyone on the internet was. Whereas, if I was the innocent victim of a pack of online misogynists . . .

'Sort of. I mean, I got death threats.' That part was true anyway, wasn't it?

She swore under her breath. 'And you reported it? Did the police help?' She shook her head. 'Of course they didn't. That is so wrong! Why should YOU be the one who has to go into hiding?' She grabbed me by the arms, practically hyperventilating. 'THIS WORLD MAKES ME SO ANGRY!'

A pair of smartly dressed French guys beside us were looking at us curiously.

'Vee, it's fine, honestly, it's not – I mean – you know.' I just wanted this to be over. If I had ever thought of telling Vee the truth, it was too late now.

'It makes me sick! So – what's your real name?'

'I'm sorry, I'd rather not say. It's easier if I just stick to Lola.'

'But you shouldn't have to do this!'

'I'd rather not talk about it,' I said, hoping she would take the hint.

'OK.' She hugged me, fiercely. A little voice inside was shrieking 'STOP!' but it was too late. Way, way too late.

'Thanks for listening,' I said. 'I hope you can understand why I haven't been, like, totally truthful.'

'Of course,' she said immediately. 'Look – about the committee.'

'What about it?'

'I was being mean about that. The thing is . . .' she sighed. 'I ran for Class Rep. Three years ago. I didn't get it. I was really upset.'

'Oh – Vee, I'm sorry. I didn't know. It's horrible when stuff like that happens.' I still vividly remembered when the Young Entrepreneurs picked Jules instead of me to be their marketing manager.

'So when you got onto the committee – and you've only been here a few weeks – I got jealous. I should have just said so earlier.'

'I didn't know,' I repeated. 'I'm really, really sorry.'

'It's OK. I'm so sorry about what happened to you, too. I'm really glad we finally talked about this.' She smiled. 'I feel so much better now.'

'Yes,' I said weakly. 'Me too.'

Chapter thirty-three

'Ah, Madame, you are going down,' said Tariq. 'But I am going up.'

'Huh?' I said. We had just collided on the staircase in the main building. My arms were full of posters for the ball, and my mind was equally preoccupied by stressing over Vee. Plus, he'd said it in French, so it took me a minute to translate it.

'It's what the Marquise de Maintenon said to Madame de Montespan,' Tariq explained, taking some excess posters from me. 'When she was replacing her as the Sun King's mistress. She got a room in a better position on the staircase at Versailles, you see. So it was a sick burn.'

'Oh, I get it.'

'Let's see?' He unrolled one of the posters I'd made. 'This is fantastic, Lola. It looks even better printed out.'

'Thanks,' I said, pleased. 'It was hard to explain "come as the meaning of your name" but I think we managed it.'

'Even the Sun King couldn't ask for more,' Tariq said. 'Though we won't be importing four hundred orange trees in tubs for our costume party. Here, I'll give you a hand.'

I passed him the Blu-Tak. 'How do you know so much about the Sun King?' I asked curiously.

'I'm doing my extended essay on him. Did you know his brother – Monsieur – went to war in full make-up, including false eyelashes?'

'No!' I laughed. 'Monsieur is a strange name. Couldn't they come up with anything better?'

'That's what the King's brother was always called. The King's sister was Madame.'

'Is that why that street near us is called Monsieur le Prince?'

'Yes! That's him.' He beamed. 'I wish someone would call me that. Wouldn't that be the coolest nickname ever? Aside from Sun King, obviously.'

I laughed. I still couldn't get over how Tariq could get away with this kind of thing – could stroll around chatting about the Sun King, and still be one of the most popular boys in the school instead of its greatest nerd. Truly they did things differently in Paris.

'That reminds me,' he was saying. 'Have you officially joined Film Club yet? Full disclosure: I'm social secretary and we need more members.'

'Tariq, how many clubs are you in?'

'Honestly, I've cut back. Just Speech and Debate, Film Club, Model UN – oh, and the fencing team.'

'The fencing team! That's very Sun King, isn't it?' I paused, picturing Tariq in a wig and breeches. He would look pretty good, actually.

We'd finished the posters now, and we were drifting towards the Mezzanine – an area that was used for small assemblies or for meetings with teachers. Once again, walking around with Tariq was a constant stream of back-slaps and high-fives. It must be exhausting being him. He helped me put up more posters and then we sat down together.

'Have you heard about the other candidate for Student Pres?' he asked. 'It's Hunter.'

'*Hunter*? Fletcher's boyfriend?' I was surprised. 'Why is he running instead of her? She's Grade Rep, after all.'

Tariq lifted his shoulders. 'It's her decision,' he said diplomatically. 'I suppose he wants to run and she doesn't. Can I tell you my policies?'

'Yes, of course.'

'Well, I'd like to get rid of plastic water bottles in the school,' he said. 'I've worked out that we go through about 10,000 bottles a year. And it takes 7 litres of water to make one plastic water bottle, so think of the waste.'

'That's unbelievable!'

'Yeah. We have water fountains but people don't use them enough. And also . . . I want to extend the school counselling service to weekends. People aren't always able to call during the week.'

'That sounds good but how would you make the teachers work weekends?'

'I wouldn't,' he said triumphantly. 'My mum knows someone who teaches psychology in the American University here. Their students would be happy to talk to students and get experience.'

'Nice,' I said, impressed.

'You think so?' he said. 'Thanks. I'd actually like to do more stuff for the boarding community but that would look bad, I think – because I'm a boarder.' I noticed that his knee was joggling frantically; he was obviously nervous. He grinned suddenly. 'So my plan is to get elected first – and then sneakily do stuff for boarders.'

'Well, you're already thinking like a politician,' I said.

We moved on to other topics, and I showed him my picture of Lenny's wall.

'Oh, *no*,' he said, recoiling. 'That is a horror show. Does he have psychological problems? Is he a Goth?'

'No, he's a git,' I said, and we both giggled.

I hadn't spoken to Tariq since my conversation with Kiyoshi. Now that I thought about it, his theory about Tariq being gay made sense.

It would explain his quick recovery from his break-up, *and* the fact that he was so friendly and unselfconscious with me. Plus – stereotypes aside – there was the excellent dress sense and the interest in French royal history. *And* he'd made brownies for the last Film Club meeting.

So why wasn't he out? Maybe it was his family – or maybe he was scared that if he came out, it would damage his chances of being elected as Student President, or whatever. Poor Tariq. Why was the world so awful?

Chapter thirty-four

Theory of Knowledge was one of my favourite classes, but also one of the hardest. It was a mixture of philosophy, reasoning and logic. Sometimes the starting-point was a question on the board; last week's was 'How do we know we are human?' Which was quite a lot to deal with on a Tuesday morning.

Ms Curtis, the teacher, was a lean, sallow American woman who had already won me over by using a video of Benedict Cumberbatch as Holmes, to illustrate the difference between deductive and inductive reasoning.

Today the question on the whiteboard was 'Is internet censorship good for society?' We spent a while discussing photos of violence and of crimes, before we got onto privacy.

'Can you ever remove photos of yourself from the internet?' Priya asked faux-casually.

We hadn't seen her much since she'd started dating her new boyfriend. Using inductive reasoning, I decided Priya was probably worried about photographs of her ending up online. I hoped not, but Tyger seemed exactly the kind of guy who would do that.

'In theory, yes – if they've been stolen, and if you have the resources to take legal action. But in practice, it's almost impossible.'

We discussed the hacking of celebrity photos, and the difference between a photo that was stolen and one that was just being used without consent.

'Wasn't there a case in Spain – a man who wanted to remove himself from the internet?' someone asked.

'Yes!' said Ms Curtis. 'He had been in debt and although he had paid it, the details of his debt kept coming up when he was googled. He was successful. Now Google allows individuals to request to remove things about themselves from search engines.'

What? How had nobody told me about this?

'Yes, Vee?'

Vee, two desks away from me, was looking as though she wanted to explode. 'But that's censorship,' she said. 'What about murderers, and rapists?'

'What about them?' Ms Curtis said, to encourage her. 'How is that different?'

'Because we need to know!'

'So it's in the public interest? Good point.' She wrote, 'Public interest,' on the board. 'Yes. But what if it's a crime that wasn't violent, and happened a long time ago? What if you shoplifted when you were seventeen and it kept coming up when you were job-hunting in your twenties? Is that good for society?'

Everyone was quiet. I half-looked around the class discreetly. Tariq wasn't saying anything, but he was doodling in his notebook and I could tell he was listening carefully.

Vee frowned, thinking it out. 'Yes,' she said eventually. 'Because if you start removing results for some people – where does it end? What if some people get their results cleaned up and some don't – how is that fair?'

Other people started talking all at once.

'Obviously each case is going to be different and has to be decided on its own merit,' Ms Curtis said. 'Let's go back to the original example – the man who paid his debt, but the story kept coming up. Who thinks he should *not* have the right to delete search results about this?'

Vee's hand shot straight up, as did about half the room's. I noticed that Tariq looked to see what everyone else was doing before raising his hand. Reluctantly, I raised my own hand, so as not to look suspicious.

'And who thinks that he *should* have the right to delete it?'

I was disappointed to see that only a quarter of the room put their hand up. I was especially disappointed in Tariq – not because of the way he'd voted, but the way he took the temperature of the room before doing so. It was true that he was a bit of a people-pleaser. But as I knew myself, nobody was perfect.

Chapter thirty-five

The next few weeks were the happiest I'd had in months.

The candles were coming out on the chestnut trees and tourists were also coming out in droves, making me feel smug that I lived here and was a real Parisian. I didn't even mind when Lenny texted me endless pictures from his school trip. Of course, he was going to Naples and Amalfi with Holly. It looked more like a celebrity honeymoon than a school trip.

Easter was early that year. I decided that, instead of going home for the break, I would stay in Jean Monnet.

'Are you sure you're OK with this?' Mum asked me for the tenth time. 'We haven't see you in so long.'

'Six weeks,' I corrected her. 'That's nothing, Mum. There are people here who haven't seen their parents in six months.'

I knew that it would be much easier to get to grips with all my work if I stayed in school. Plus, it had taken me this long to settle in to Jean Monnet; I didn't want to go back and then have to settle in all over again.

But there was another reason. For the first time in months, I was actually feeling OK about myself. I wasn't a horrible person; I was doing worthwhile things. I was still drowning in work, but I felt like I was actually learning things and not just cramming for exams. I loved being on the committee. I had friends. Even if half of my friends had nothing to say to the other half, I still had people to hang out with, who I liked and who liked me. And if I went home, I was scared that all of that would fall apart.

Vee was completely fine with me now that she knew my secret – or thought she did. She and Kiyoshi were in denial about study, so most afternoons we would hire Vélib bikes and cycle along the Canal Saint Martin, or go and browse in the flea markets in Clignancourt. We also went to see a film in the Pagoda, a cinema that was built to look like a miniature Chinese pavilion. Vee knew so many interesting nooks and crannies, I realised I was seeing a side of Paris that I never would have seen as a tourist.

She also helped me refresh my wardrobe with several cool new things – vintage Levi's with rips in the knee, culottes, and a black sweater with studs. They definitely made me look more like a Lola than like my old self.

'Are you sure I can carry them off?' I asked Vee.

'Definitely!' she said. 'Especially with your hair. It is so cool. Have you ever thought about doing a nose ring?'

'I'm not totally sure about that,' I said doubtfully. 'I'm getting a bit sick of my hair, too.' The roots were showing more and more, and it was making me look really pale. But it still seemed a little risky to go back to my original brown.

We also talked endlessly about Kiyoshi's crush on Marco Agnelli. Marco had invited him to like his private Instagram, and their Snapchat streaks were out of this world, apparently. And yet they never spoke in real life. It all sounded very confusing.

'It's like I'm his Tamagotchi,' Kiyoshi complained.

I went out a few times with Tariq and Fletcher, who were stuck here over the holidays too. The ostensible reason was to do party planning, but we generally didn't do much of that. Our usual haunt was the Place de la Contrescarpe in the Latin Quarter, a beautiful, lively cobbled square with trees and a fountain, ringed with cafés with red awnings. It was off the rue Mouffetard, which was full of bars and crepe stalls that were thronged at all hours – another busy, bustling student street that I loved.

'Why aren't there places like this in London?' I said with a sigh one evening towards the end of the holidays.

'What about that famous South Bank?' said Tariq. 'That's pretty good.'

'Oh yeah!' said Fletcher, who was sitting with us. 'That's in *Four Weddings and a Funeral*.'

'That's true,' I said. I had a sudden memory of last summer, when they put giant deckchairs outside the National Theatre, and Nisha and Ellie and I sat out there all day listening to music and filming ourselves and being silly. To drive the thought away, I said quickly, 'But the South Bank is always so crowded. Paris is much prettier.'

'See, that's the difference between the French and the English,' said Tariq. 'The French think France is the best

153

country in the world. The English think England is the worst.'

'I don't think that,' I said, laughing.

'Oh, and the Americans,' Tariq added, looking teasingly at Fletcher. 'They think America's the best country in the world. That's why they get so confused in France.'

I looked at Fletcher, wondering how she would react to that one.

'No we don't,' she said, looking indignant. After a beat, she added, 'We think we're the *only* country in the world.'

We all laughed at that and I thought how Fletcher could occasionally surprise me by having a bit more of an edge than I'd expected.

'What's that noise?' Tariq said, hearing an alert.

'Oh, it's my Inspalert,' said Fletcher. 'It sends me inspirational messages.' She looked faintly embarrassed. 'This one says: Today is the first day of the rest of your life.'

Looking around the square, with its trees lit up by fairy lights and its splashing fountain, I thought; this *is* the first day of the rest of my life. My plan had worked. I was in a different place, I was hanging out with different people. I even looked different, with my hair and my new clothes. Not even Vee had found me out. I really did it. I had left Delilah behind and I was Lola now.

Chapter thirty-six

'Hey babe!' a voice said above us.

It was Fletcher's boyfriend, Hunter, and the other identikit couple. I knew they were called Riley and August, but I honestly didn't know which was which.

I also knew that Hunter was the other person running for president of the Student Council. I would have expected him and Tariq to be a little icy with each other but apparently not.

'You ready for next week, man?' he said to Tariq. Next week were the hustings when the two candidates would announce their policies.

'Ready as I'll ever be,' said Tariq, grinning. 'Are *you* ready?'

'Bring it,' said Hunter.

It was not like that with me and Nisha, when I was made Junior Prefect and she wasn't. Maybe that rivalry was easier for boys. It seemed almost expected of them, whereas girls were expected to get along.

'You guys want to join us?' Fletcher asked Hunter.

'No, I'm pretty beat. Let's head home, babe,' he replied.

Fletcher got up and started putting on her jacket.

'Let me give you something for the hot chocolate,' she said to Tariq. 'Oh, wait. I need to get cash. I'll find a machine.'

'Fletcher!' Tariq said. 'It's fine. I can buy you a hot chocolate.'

'No!' she said. 'I can't let you pay for me. Wait. I bet I have it somewhere.' She started rootling through the bottom of her bag. I looked at her boyfriend.

'Sorry, babe – I got nothing,' he said serenely.

'Fletcher,' Tariq said sternly. 'I'm going to get really quite annoyed at you, if you don't let me buy you one measly hot chocolate. Come on. You're being ridiculous.'

'Yes, come on Fletcher,' I added. 'It's much easier if we just pay.'

'No! I can't let you pay for me!'

After a lot more wrangling, she finally agreed as long as she could get Tariq back next time. It was so awfully awkward, I was relieved when they eventually left. Fletcher was one of those people who could never, ever let you do her a favour. I'd seen her leave class and go back to her room to get a pen, rather than borrow one. She meant it as a nice thing, of course, but it was actually maddening.

Once they were gone, I turned to Tariq. 'Is it really bad that I can't remember which is Riley and which is August?'

'You're a monster. Riley's the girl,' he said, grinning.

'Hunter is . . .' I trailed off. Did I know Tariq well

156

enough to bitch about someone with him? Would he even be willing to do that or was he too diplomatic?

'He's pretty selfish,' he said, frankly. 'Fletcher's too good for him. But it always seems to work out that way, doesn't it?'

I nodded, relieved that Tariq was human enough to be mean about someone on occasion.

It had started to rain – hitting off the fountain in big splashes and running in rivulets down the windows of the café. The red and yellow lights of the cafés opposite us became distorted in the raindrops. I knew Tariq would have an umbrella; he always did.

'I know everyone complains about rain,' I said. 'But I secretly quite like it.'

'This isn't proper rain,' he said. 'You should come to Lahore in the monsoon season. It's like nothing else you've ever seen. It's sheets and sheets of water, descending from the sky, like it's going to obliterate the earth. But afterwards . . . all the dust is gone, everything is green and fresh and you can see each individual drop sparkling on each leaf, and there's this smell of freshness and green and life . . . I really miss it. Lawrence Gardens in the monsoon – that's one of the top places on earth.'

'What's Lawrence Gardens?'

'It's also called Bagh-e-Jinnah – it's named after the founder of Pakistan. It's the most beautiful park – you can walk for miles and miles, under these enormous trees. We lived near there when I was a kid.'

'Did you used to cycle there?'

'No – we had a driver.' Seeing my face, he said, almost embarrassed, 'It's not that unusual back home.'

'Do you think you'll go back to live there?' I asked. 'Oh, sorry, you said. After university.'

He bit his nail. 'That was my plan,' he said. 'But I don't know. If I go to university in the UK – which I'd like to – I'll have lived abroad for longer than I lived at home. To be honest with you, I feel like I'm becoming kind of deracinated. I'm even forgetting my Urdu.'

'Really? Didn't you grow up speaking Urdu?'

'Of course, partly. But we've always spoken English at home.'

'Can you teach me some?'

'Sure.' He taught me 'Hello' and 'Thank you'. Then he said, 'You really are a language geek, aren't you?'

'You have no idea how geeky.' I hesitated, then admitted, 'I invented my own language.'

'Your own language? You mean, like pig Latin?'

'*No,*' I said, indignant. 'It's a proper one.'

'What does it sound like?'

'Well . . . it's a Romance language. Which means it's like French or Italian, but it's also got borrowings from English. So, "I want" is *Ya windeth*. "Do you want" is *Deja ta windeth*.'

'*Deja ta windeth* . . . so the verb stays the same?'

'Oh yeah, no conjugation. Much easier. So "*Deja ta windeth a eo?*" means "Do you want to go?" '

'*Deja ta windeth a eo,*' he repeated. 'Is that right?'

'That's it – that's good! You're picking it up.'

'*Deja ta windeth a eo*. I like it,' Tariq said. 'Can you teach me more?'

'OK, but I warn you, there's very few native speakers. Just me and my little brother really.'

'Does it have a name? Your language?'

'It's called, um, Lolese.' I had to think quickly because obviously I couldn't tell him it was Delilish.

The rain had stopped outside. We sat there for a while, idly people-watching.

'We should go soon,' I said, lazily.

'In a bit,' he said.

I noticed that almost all the men who went by were wearing long cotton scarves – it was a total craze among Parisian men. I was going to ask Tariq what that was all about when I realised *he* was wearing a long cotton scarf.

'I like your trench coat, by the way,' Tariq said. 'Actually your whole outfit is very cute. You look like a French girl.'

'Really? Thanks.' After seeing so many of them for weeks, I had finally caved and bought one in a shop on the rue de Seine, and I absolutely loved it. It wasn't a baggy vintage one like Vee's; it was fitted and belted. I had also bought a little brown suede skirt – not unlike Priscilla's – and a black polo neck, both of which I was wearing, with my old leather boots.

Weirdly, I had noticed that I tended to dress in a much more preppy way when I was around Tariq than when I was out with Vee and Kiyoshi. I didn't know why that was – maybe because I was worried that Vee would think I looked like a preppy clone. Or that Tariq would be

159

embarrassed to be seen with me in my crazier outfits. Which was stupid. I should just wear what I wanted. Whatever that was.

The waiter came by to see if we wanted another drink, and I shook my head.

'It's almost nine,' Tariq said reluctantly. 'We'd better go.'

We were having such a good time I hadn't even noticed. Ten was our absolute latest curfew, but we had to be signed in specially if it was after nine. Although, even if it had been three a.m. and we'd been steaming drunk, I was fairly sure that Tariq could have sweet-talked the staff on reception.

Chapter thirty-seven

'I'm really hungry,' Tariq said suddenly. 'Do you mind if we stop for a crepe?'

'No, of course. I've never actually had one yet.'

Tariq stopped dead still. 'Hold on,' he said. 'You've never had a CREPE? How is that even possible? What have you been doing with yourself? How long have you been in Paris?'

'A while?' I said, laughing. 'Give me a break! I've been busy.'

He clasped his hands to his head. 'This is a disaster. We don't even have time to take you to the best one. Never mind. We'll try Michel's. Hopefully the queue won't be too bad.'

He marched me towards a busy stall, beside a souvenir shop, where two guys were working diligently on two round, metal bases, sizzling butter onto them, then pouring the batter on and swirling it into round circles with a sort of metal trowel. It was emitting the smells that had been haunting my dreams ever since I'd come to Paris.

'So that's where that smell's coming from!' I said. 'I didn't realise.'

'This gets worse and worse,' said Tariq. 'Do you want Nutella or *jambon fromage* – that's ham and cheese?'

'I know what *jambon fromage* means,' I said, poking him.

'Well I don't know, Lola. I can't assume anything, if you've never even had a crepe.'

'It's got to be Nutella, doesn't it? Wait, let me give you some money.'

He shook his head vehemently. 'I absolutely insist. This is your first crepe – let me buy it for you. It's the least I can do after such a terrible omission.'

He ordered in rapid French, and we waited while Michel whipped together our two crepes with Nutella.

'Now,' said Tariq. 'I defy you to tell me that's not the best thing you've ever tasted.'

I took a bite. Insanely gooey chocolate and the soft, salty sweetness of the crepe . . . I nodded speechlessly.

'May that be the first of many,' said Tariq. 'Right. I'm not going to be able to talk for a bit.'

'Me either,' I said, through a mouthful. We walked away from the stall, stuffing ourselves in companionable silence.

'I thought nowhere could beat Lahore for street food, when we moved here,' he said. 'But I'm prepared to admit, the crepes are pretty good.'

I took a last regretful bite. 'That was easily one of the best things I've done since I arrived here. We'll have to do it again.'

'I'm free any time.'

'Really? You seem pretty busy to me.'

'Not really. You know Nicolas and Patrick don't board . . . and Patrick is booked up with Rose now that they're dating. So I'm often at a loose end in the evenings. Crying onto my laptop, begging someone to save me from my extended essay.'

'You, at a loose end?' I laughed. 'Come on. You can't go down the corridor without saying hello to four hundred people.'

'Yes, well. You can have six hundred friends on Facebook and nobody to have dinner with.'

I was quite struck by this. Maybe he did get lonely sometimes – as impossible as it seemed. And it was true that there was a difference between friends online, and friends in real life.

Thinking about this made me remember Kiyoshi, and his problems with Marco Agnelli. I wondered if I should get a guy's perspective on it.

'Tariq,' I said. 'What do you think it means when a guy messages you all the time . . . but in real life you hardly speak?'

He frowned. 'It can mean anything, I suppose. He might be shy?'

'He's definitely shy.'

'Well – do you like him?'

'Oh, no, it's not me! It's happening to a friend.' I laughed. 'I know that sounds like I'm lying but it really is. Just a friend.'

'Who?'

'I can't say. But what would you do, if you were my friend?'

After a pause, he said. 'I don't know. I suppose I'd be wondering – shouldn't he be asking you out? Or at least spending time with you – getting to know you? Properly, not just online.' He hesitated. 'I mean why wouldn't he want to do that?'

'That's a good point. Thanks, Tariq,' I said. Impulsively, I squeezed his arm. 'You're a great friend.'

He smiled, though he looked a bit distracted. Maybe the arm squeeze had been too much. Oh dear. He was probably worried that I was developing a crush on *him*.

'Have you been in touch with Priscilla lately?'

'With Priscilla? Yes. Here, give me that.' He balled up my crepe wrapper and put it in a recycling bin, along with his. 'I haven't told many people this, but . . . we've broken up.'

'Oh! I'm sorry.' I added cautiously, 'What happened?'

'It's the distance really. We were talking about visiting over Easter, but it just wasn't practical when we both have so much work to do. And our parents aren't about to start shelling out for transatlantic flights.'

I nodded. This was all very sensible and practical. But I couldn't help wondering if the real reason for their break-up was more to do with Tariq liking boys. The way he wolfed down his crepe didn't suggest he was particularly heartbroken.

It was so sad, if that was the case. Tariq was probably one of my favourite people here, and it was such a pity he couldn't come out, even to me. But then, I was hardly one to talk.

Chapter thirty-eight

I missed the holidays as soon as they were over, but it was nice to walk back into the cafeteria, on that first day back, feeling like a proper student here instead of an interloper.

I had been thinking, over the Easter holidays, about how crazy it was that I kept my friends in such different boxes. Maybe I should try and mix them up more? But I changed my mind after Vee and Tariq had a full-on argument during Theory of Knowledge. The question on the board was 'Should we vote?' Vee, unsurprisingly, said no, because politicians were all the same. Tariq tried to keep calm but ended up accusing her of first-world privilege and complacency. I kept my head down, but I decided that some things, like all my friends getting on, just weren't meant to be.

The big excitement of the first week back at school was the hustings meeting, where the two rivals for Student President would give a speech to the entire school. Vee had threatened to boycott it, but had finally agreed to come along when Kiyoshi had pointed out that there would be the opportunity to ask provocative questions.

Tariq was up first. I would have been sick with nerves, but he looked utterly relaxed. It was odd to think that this guy – this star of the school – was the same person who had asked me for advice about laundry, and bought me a crepe and learned basic Delilish.

'Thanks, everyone,' he said, once everyone had quietened down. 'I'm so honoured to be running for this position. Jean Monnet isn't just a school to me – it's my home. And you guys are my family.'

'Vomit,' said Vee, beside me.

She looked more approving, though, when he announced his policies – the bottled water ban and the extension of counselling hours.

'Those are not terrible ideas,' she said.

'Mmn,' I said, shrinking down in my seat. One of the things you had to accept about Vee was that she had absolutely no indoor voice. I was relieved when he eventually stepped down, to enthusiastic applause.

'This should be interesting,' murmured Kiyoshi, as Hunter stepped up.

'OK, guys,' he said. 'You're busy people so I'll keep this short. The first thing I have to say is: everybody be chill. I am NOT here to take away your bottled water. Your Evian and Vittel are safe with me!'

There was quite a scattering of applause, especially from the lower years.

'Second thing,' he said. 'Once I am president, I will personally guarantee that we have pancakes for breakfast on Mondays, Wednesdays *and* Fridays. Not crepes, pancakes. With bacon AND genuine maple syrup!'

166

There was wild applause for this. 'Can he actually guarantee that?' I asked Kiyoshi, who shrugged.

'If the Student Council back him up, probably. Two years ago the president introduced giant cookies. Big hit.'

'Lastly,' Hunter said, holding up a hand. 'I was very disappointed that this year's Entertainment Committee – led by Tariq here – decided to cancel our Venetian Masked Ball in favour of a costume party, which honestly, sounds pretty lame-o. And I know that everyone in IB One and Two was disappointed too. When I am president, I will make sure that it happens. Ladies, you SHALL go to the ball!'

I gasped. 'That's appalling! That's not what happened!'

'Doesn't matter,' said Vee. 'The crowd loves it.'

The whole room was applauding wildly. Up on the platform, Tariq's face was set in a smile, but I could tell he was furious. Mr Gerardo was speaking quietly to Ms Curtis, who shook her head.

'He'll get a chance to rebut that, won't he?' I said. 'In the debate?'

'There is no debate,' Kiyoshi said. 'They just announce their policies and that's that. And they're not allowed to canvass either. No posters, nothing. This was their chance.'

I couldn't believe it. 'But that's not what happened! The teacher explained why it was a bad idea and we all voted on it.'

'Is he really going to take away our sparkling water?' Kiyoshi said, looking worried. 'I know it's bad for the environment, but I literally don't think I can get through the IB without it.'

And it was true that lots of younger kids were swarming madly around Hunter, who was being patted on the back by his buddies. I noticed Fletcher leave the hall alone, her face stony. I wondered how she'd felt about Hunter calling the Spring Ball, which she was helping to organise, 'lame-o.'

The whole thing made me realise something. I had no desire any more to stand up there, the way Tariq and Hunter just had, and battle it out to be in charge. The whole thing just seemed too stressful.

Tariq was leaving the stage, with Patrick and Nicolas beside him. He had a lot less of a crowd around him than Hunter did. I tried to catch his eye, but obviously he was distracted.

'I'm really sorry,' I said to him, as he went by us. 'That was a really dick move from Hunter.'

He flashed me a quick smile. 'Not at all. It was all good fun.'

'Do you want to—'

I was about to ask him if he wanted to get lunch, but he was barely listening. 'Thanks for coming!' He patted me on the shoulder, and then he was gone, with the other two.

I supposed that he wanted to get away and lick his wounds. But why not say so? Why be so . . . fake about it? That was politics for you, I suppose.

Chapter thirty-nine

Thump. Thump. Thump. What was that?

It was Friday night, four days after the hustings, and I was trying to do my French homework – an essay on Fair Trade, or Commerce Equitable, that would have been difficult enough in English. I was also being driven nuts by that steady thump. I went out to the corridor, but there wasn't a sound.

Then I heard that thump again. It was coming from Fletcher's room.

'Fletcher?' I knocked on the door. 'What's up?'

'Come in,' she croaked. Her voice sounded foggy, as if she had a cold.

The room was dark, and she was lying in bed, a pile of crumpled tissues beside her.

'Are you OK?' I said stupidly.

'I'm sorry to bother you. I just need—' She sneezed, then burst into tears.

Panicking, I said, 'Don't worry! Should I get Susannah?' Susannah was the teaching assistant who was responsible for the female boarders.

Fletcher shook her head. 'No. I just have a bad cold. And I need a tampon,' she said. 'I would ask the other girls but . . . Mette uses those non-applicator ones and I just can't,' she finished, looking embarrassed.

'Don't worry! I've got a box. All flavours.'

I ran next door. Luckily, I had stocked up in a paranoid fashion before coming over, although I knew rationally that they did have these things in France. Fletcher went off to the bathroom, leaving me to look around her room, which was not in a good place. Piles of tissues; cough sweets; an empty bottle of Evian and various aggressive-looking American flu remedies. I didn't even know she was sick. There was also a chocolate bar and a John Meyer CD – these must be desperate times.

'You poor thing,' I said when she got back. 'You must be feeling rotten. Can I get you anything else?'

She got back into bed, looking grey and shaken. 'No, it's fine. Please tell me how much I owe you – I'll pay you for these.'

'Fletcher, seriously. It's fine. Do you need some more water?'

'No, honestly, I'm good.' She coughed, then sneezed, and looked around for a tissue. I went out and came back with some tissues from my room, plus a bottle of water.

'Where is Hunter, anyway?' I asked. 'Why isn't he looking after you?'

'We broke up.'

Oh, no. This explained the chocolate and the John Meyer CD.

'I'm really sorry,' I said. 'Look, let me make you some tea with honey.'

She hesitated.

'OK,' she said in a low voice. 'Thanks.' Then her lip trembled again. 'I'm sorry to be a nuisance.'

'It's fine! Just don't apologise!'

I ran down to the vending machines and got her some more bottles of water. Then I made a cup of tea, adding some of Mette's honey from the kitchen. Back in Fletcher's room, I got her to agree to let me tidy a few things away – I knew the mess would be driving her crazy, as it would me. Soon her room was looking much better, as was she, after chugging down an entire litre of water.

'Thanks,' she said. 'that's one of the worst things about boarding, isn't it? Being sick without your family around.'

'Whereabouts is your family?' I asked.

I meant 'which part of America' but she said, 'They're in Kazakhstan. My parents both work for Habitat for Humanity. That's why I'm here – so that we can meet in Europe instead of flying transatlantic all the time.'

It was a sign of how long I'd been in Jean Monnet that this story actually sounded pretty normal. I wondered what Vee would say to that: she'd been convinced that Fletcher's father was part of the dropping-bombs-on-villagers brigade.

'What happened with Hunter?' I asked tentatively. 'You don't have to talk about it if you don't want to.'

She shook her head. 'You can probably guess. I

mean, the whole school heard him describe the Spring Ball – which I've been working on for weeks – as "lame-o".'

I winced.

'But anyway . . . I don't want to bore you with all this stuff,' she said, looking worried. 'You've got homework to do, I bet.'

'It's fine, honestly.'

'And let me know what I owe you for those,' she added, indicating the tissues. 'I'll replace them.'

'Fletcher—' Suddenly my irritation took over. 'It's just a tissue, for God's sake! I know you're trying to be nice but it's really, really annoying!'

She looked at me and burst into tears.

'Oh. Gosh, I'm so sorry!' I ran over and gave her the world's most awkward hug. What was I thinking? I was a monster.

Through tears, she said, 'That's what Hunter always says about me.'

What a prince. He had a point, but still.

'It's Tariq I feel bad for, really,' she said. 'He's worked so hard on figuring out some positive plans, and then Hunter comes in with his stupid pancakes and everyone goes crazy for it.'

'You don't think he'll win, do you?'

'I don't know. Our year will vote for Tariq, and probably the IB Two as well. But the rest of the school, I'm not so sure. Have you talked to Tariq?'

'No.' It was true that ever since the hustings, he'd been very elusive. 'Want me to see if he's home?'

172

'I'm too sick to talk to anyone.' She looked miserable again. 'And anyway, he's bound to be out. Staying in on a Friday night is like death to Tariq.'

'Look, why don't we watch an episode of *The Office*?' I suggested.

'The US *Office*?' Fletcher asked hopefully. 'I mean, the UK one is funny too. But—'

'I know. The US one is happier.'

It was a particularly funny one, where Kevin makes a giant chilli and spills it all over the floor. Fletcher laughed so much she said it hurt, but in a good way.

'Thanks, Lola,' she added, as I got up to leave. 'I hope I can do you a favour soon . . .'

'Honestly, Fletcher, I think you should start asking for more favours, not less.'

A thoughtful expression crossed her face. 'In that case. Will you be my jogging partner? Or at least try it?'

Jogging?

'No. Sorry, but I've tried it before and it was impossible. I'm not cut out for it.'

'We'll start slow,' she said. 'I promise. One minute slow jog, one minute walking. Just try it once, and if you don't like it I will never make you do it again, I promise.'

She might be too nice but she was also very tenacious. 'Fine,' I said. 'I'll try it.'

Chapter forty

Talking to Fletcher about her family had made me think of mine. I felt really guilty: it had been ages since I'd talked to them – properly, not just messages. I decided to Skype them there and then.

Lenny answered. It had only been about ten days since I'd last seen him on screeen. But he looked older. Not just his face; his whole expression. And was that *stubble* I was seeing?

'Sup,' he said. 'Should I get Mum? She's in the bath, but for you she would drip.'

'No, wait – hang on! How are you? How was your school trip?'

'It was OK.'

'What do you mean, OK?' I said. 'It looked like a honeymoon, not a school trip. Seriously – you're living the dream.'

'Living the dream?' Lenny said. 'I'm not living any flipping dream.'

'What do you mean?' Now I was indignant. 'Was I imagining the Segway – and the chocolate croissants

– *and* the staying out til all hours? Not to mention you've destroyed my room, and you have a *girlfriend* now? What am I missing?'

'Chocolate croissants?' said Lenny. 'You seriously think a few chocolate croissants can make up for all the other stuff that's happening?'

'What other stuff?' My heart thumped. 'Are Mum and Dad fighting?'

'Um, of *course*. When they're not micro-managing everything I do.'

'Like what?'

'Like – we have dinner together *every* night. At the table, *not* on the sofa.'

'Oh God, really?' That sounded intense. Dinner at the table was normally only Christmas and Sundays.

'And they make me tell them my *best* and *worst* moment of the day.' He sounded full of horror. 'And they look at my internet search history every day. I'm only allowed my phone for an hour every evening. It's like living in a police state.'

'Come on. A police state? You've got a girlfriend!'

'Yes,' said Lenny. 'And I'm not allowed to tell her where my sister is.'

'But – why does she . . .'

'Why does she care? Because it's weird! It's like we've disappeared you! You can't just go off somewhere and have people not ask where you went. It doesn't work like that.'

Confused, I said, 'But . . . Mum and Dad are telling people I'm in Paris. Can't you just say that?'

'No! Because you told me not to!'

'Oh.' I hadn't expected that Lenny would even remember me asking him that. 'Well – you can tell her. Just don't tell her why I left.'

'You don't think she already knows?'

'I suppose,' I said, awkwardly. 'I mean course I do. I just don't want people here knowing, is all.'

'Delilah. They're going to find out eventually. You're in Paris, not on the moon.'

I blinked. Was that really Lenny talking? Suddenly, he sounded like Dad.

'But it's too late,' I said. 'It's too late to tell anyone here. I'm so steeped in blood that returning were as tedious as going back.'

'Steeped in blood? What the hell have you done now?'

'I was joking! It's from *Macbeth*.'

'Very funny. I've got to go.' And he logged off, without waiting for my reply.

Chapter forty-one

That night, I couldn't sleep. My mind was such a jumble of thoughts – about Lenny being angry with me, as well as him growing up so fast and me missing it all; about whether I would ever go back to being Delilah again; and about poor Fletcher, Tariq and the Student President election. I sighed aloud, tossing and turning, until I got out of bed. Restless, I walked to the window. There was a full moon. I turned my light on, and decided to try to read.

A few minutes later, there was a knock at my door. I opened it, half-expecting it to be Fletcher.

It was Tariq. I blinked at the sight of him; half-swaying in the doorway, dark hair ruffled over his forehead. If I didn't know better, I'd have said he was . . . Drunk?

'Pause. Record scratch,' he said. 'You're probably wondering how I got here!'

I bundled him inside quickly before anyone heard him.

'So sorry to call by so late. I just saw your light was on,' he said. He was obviously being careful to speak distinctly. 'And I thought I'd see if you wanted to come up on the roof, for some fresh air.'

'Tariq! Keep your voice down. What roof?'

'The roof of the *school*,' he said patiently. 'Look.' He produced a key. 'The key to the old fire escape.'

I knew I should shut him up and persuade him back to his room, but I could tell there would be no peace unless I let him. Instead I found myself pulling on my dressing-gown, and my monster slippers.

Tariq looked at them. 'Oh, Lola. Are you eight?' He started to giggle.

'Shhh,' I said. 'Come on. Let's go on the roof, if we're going.'

My heart was in my mouth as we tip-toed along the corridor, keeping to the edges to avoid creaks. Tariq made a huge racket unlocking the door, but miraculously, no one appeared.

'Is is safe?' I asked, creaking cautiously up the metal stairs. They were very steep, and very close to the edge.

'You are going to love the view,' Tariq said.

'The view of my life flashing in front of me as I crash down these stairs? *Oh*.'

All of Paris lay spread out before us. The Eiffel Tower was sending out its searchlight, catching all the slanted grey rooftops of the seventh, sixth and fifth arrondissements, under the light of the full moon. Behind us, the Panthéon was lit up in all its grey glory, and turning the other way, across the Seine, I could see Notre Dame and the tiny white dome of the Sacré Coeur.

'Look over there. You can see the Arc de Triomphe.'

178

I shook my head. 'This is just incredible. Why have I never been here before?' I said.

'Um, because it's completely forbidden and I don't want to get kicked out of school?'

That made me laugh out loud. 'You're not going to get kicked out of school. Anyway,' I added teasingly, 'your dad is a diplomat, isn't he? Couldn't you just get him to make a phone call?'

'I don't think you understand,' he said. 'The whole point of being a diplomat is *not* to make trouble. And avoid headlines. "Pakistani ambassador's son in drink-fuelled rooftop escapade". That kind of thing.'

He went over to one of the eaves, where there was an old cushion as a sort of makeshift seat. People had obviously been up here before.

'Sorry,' he said, 'I'm a little drunk.'

I sat down beside him, leaning my back on the tall window eave. I was tempted to say, 'I would never have guessed' but I didn't think he would get the sarcasm right now. 'Where have you been?'

'With Nicolas,' Tariq said. 'Drinking whisky. Trying to forget the car crash of the other day.'

'It wasn't a car crash. Hunter is a dimwit, Tariq. Nobody is going to vote for him, or his pancakes.'

'I'm not so sure. People like pancakes. And maybe they don't want to have their Vittel taken away. Or their Evian, or their Badoit. I *know* how the French feel about mineral water.' He was talking to himself now. 'Why did I have to go all out on that? Why didn't I have some fun policies?'

'I think it's a really good idea!'

'I looked like a complete killjoy. Not to mention the ball. I'm like the Grinch that stole Christmas.'

'But that was a complete lie! I'll tell people that's not what happened.'

He looked so utterly miserable that I searched desperately for a way to cheer him up. 'Look. It's just a student election. I mean, really – is it really the end of the world if you don't win? Really?'

'I don't know,' he said indistinctly.

I felt his head jerk abruptly onto my shoulder.

'Tariq –' I lifted my hand to push it off, but then I stopped. Because having his head on my shoulder felt nice. It shouldn't have, but it did.

'Can I tell you a secret?' he said.

I was a bit worried now. Should he really be telling me this when he was drunk? But maybe this was the only time he *could* tell me.

'When I was little, I used to organise my Sylvanian Family animals into a parliament, and hold parliamentary debates with them.' A minute later, he said, 'Lola? It's not *that* funny.'

I was laughing so hard, it was a while before I could say, 'It is, you know.'

'Ow.' He sat up, disturbed by all my hysteria. Then he collapsed back down again, lying sideways this time – with his head in my lap.

I froze, my hand half-raised. Then I brought it down to rest softly on his head. Without even letting myself think about it, I stroked his head, softly.

'That's nice,' he muttered.

180

His hair felt just as soft and touchable as it looked. I allowed my hand to travel over his head, not thinking of anything.

'Who was your Sylvanian President?'

'A squirrel.'

I kept stroking his hair. Now I was noticing things like his strong eyebrows, his beautiful nose and his amazing fan of eyelashes that spread out over his cheek.

'Are you awake?' I said softly.

His eyes stayed closed.

'You know,' I said quietly, 'I did something embarrassing too, but it was much worse than playing Sylvanian families.'

Silence.

I continued, 'I did something stupid on the internet . . . I said something very stupid. And I became notorious. So, that's sort of why I'm here.'

I breathed out slowly. Just saying that out loud – even to someone who was asleep – was massive. I looked down, braced for more questions – which I wouldn't answer.

No reply. He was out for the count.

The minutes went by, as I looked at the beautiful view around me, and the even more beautiful boy. We couldn't stay here all night – tempting as it was. The trouble was, he was fast asleep. I would have to wake him. Any minute now . . .

'Boo!' Tariq said suddenly, sitting up.

'Aagh! Shut *up*! You're going to wake the whole school!' I pushed him away, heart pounding. He was sitting up and laughing.

181

'Sorry,' he said, grinning.

Then his smile faded and he pulled back, as if suddenly realising what he'd been doing. The moment became intensely awkward. We looked at each other in the half-dark until suddenly I couldn't look any more.

'We should go to bed,' I said. 'It's really late.'

He nodded, and came down the stairs after me without saying a word, and walked to my door where we said an awkward, fast goodbye.

Chapter forty-two

Twelve hours later, I was still in a daze – trying to read up on French grammar, but simultaneously trying to figure out what on earth had happened with Tariq the other night. I had never thought of him that way before, ever. And I knew that he would never think of me that way. Which meant that I had behaved in a really creepy way, by stroking his hair. What if he thought I liked him? He would be so freaked-out, especially since he would think I thought he was straight . . . I bit my pen, groaning in mortification.

'Lola?' There was a knock on my door.

'It's just me,' said Fletcher, bouncing up and down on her toes. She was dressed in her running outfit.

'Oh no,' I said.

'I promise, it'll be fun. Just try it once – that's all I'm asking.'

I had hoped I could plead lack of proper gear, but Fletcher said my trainers would be just fine. I grumbled and sighed myself into my clothes, and we went down the stairs and out the front door.

'I'm not a runner,' I warned her.

'I know, I know,' Fletcher said, ignoring me.

I started off at my usual pace, dreading how unpleasant this was going to be.

'Wait!' she said.

'What?'

'Slow it right down! If you go too fast at the start, you'll burn out. Think one pace up from slo-mo.'

'OK,' I said, amused at how bossy she sounded, compared to her usual self. Not bossy. Confident.

Slowly, slowly we jogged towards the Jardin du Luxembourg, and went in through the great gold-topped black railings. Fletcher didn't seem remotely bothered by all the people who had to dodge out of our way. She just kept to her ultra-slow pace, while she told me about her family. Her parents lived in Astana, which was the capital of Kazakhstan, along with her eight-year-old sister, who was adopted from the Congo two years ago.

'It must be hard to keep in touch?'

'It is. But I call them as often as I can,' she said. 'I email them, I send them pictures . . . I don't want to regret anything with my parents.'

I was really stunned by this. It seemed such a mature thing to say – I'd never heard any of my friends talk about their parents like that. I was still thinking about it when we got onto the topic of Hunter and their break-up.

'The thing is,' she said, as we turned down another gravel path, 'I was actually thinking of running for Student Pres. Not because I really wanted to all that much, but I thought it was important that a girl should run.'

'Good for you. Why didn't you?'

'Hunter! He told me not to! He said it would be way too much work, with the SATs and everything, and it would mean we couldn't go away for weekends and stuff. And then he put his own name in.'

'Without even telling you?' I panted. While Fletcher was able to talk in a completely normal voice, I sounded like I was having a heart attack.

'Exactly. I'm such an idiot, I believed him when he said he'd had a sudden change of heart and just emailed his application in the middle of the night. I was annoyed, but I thought it would be petty to break up over something like that. I thought we could work through it.' Her pretty face darkened. 'But then, in the hustings . . . he *knows* why we had to cancel the ball, but he twisted the truth to use it against me. I've never felt so betrayed or humiliated in all my life.'

I just shook my head. Partly because there were no words to say what a dick he was, but partly because I could barely breathe.

'You know what else?'

Saying 'No,' was beyond me so I shook my head.

'When I was thinking of running, he said, "They'll never elect a girl." And it's true. There has never been a female Student Pres.' She shook her head. 'And there won't be one this year either. I can't believe I was that stupid! Oh, sorry. I speeded up.' She grinned at me. 'Being angry always makes me run faster.'

We slowed down – thank God. We were nearly at the end of this avenue. Surely we would stop here or at least turn round? Only my pride was preventing me from collapsing on the floor.

'You were right to dump him,' I said, once I'd recovered my breath.

'Do you think so? Riley and August think I'm being really unsupportive.'

'They're crazy. Really,' I panted. I was beginning to see stars.

Fletcher glanced at me. 'OK, let's cool the jets. That was fifteen minutes. Well done!'

'Only fifteen minutes? It felt like hours.'

'Yup. Which means, you jogged over a mile! Awesome!' She held up her hand for a high-five. 'Now let's walk for a bit.'

I limped along, realising that this was further into the park than I had ever come by myself. The chestnut trees were putting out soft, green leaves. People were sunbathing on the special green metal seats, which came in two varieties; upright and reclining. An ice-cream seller had replaced the man who used to sell chestnuts.

I had barely recovered, when Fletcher started to jog again.

'Again?' I said, protesting. 'But we already jogged.'

'You can do it! You're strong!' she chirped back, leaving me no option but to follow her along. She kept the pace really slow, as before, and I started to notice something really strange. It was getting *easier*.

'It's funny,' I said breathlessly. 'I always found that running was easy at first, but then I'm knackered after ten minutes.'

Fletcher started laughing. 'Knackered? What the heck does that mean? Tired? Well, you will be tired, but you can run for longer, because you're not burning out.'

We jogged on for a while, and my feet and arms began to settle into a rhythm. I was getting used to it. It almost felt good.

'Anyway,' said Fletcher. 'The sad thing is . . . I do miss Hunter. Isn't that weird? And I'm bummed out that I have to go to the ball alone. Who are you going with?'

'Um, no one,' I said, feeling worried. 'I mean, just Vee and Kiyoshi probably. Do we have to go with someone?'

'Well, yeah. I mean, you don't notice once you're actually at the ball. But all the couples' names go up on the Facebook page, a few weeks before. So it's really obvious if you're not going with anyone.'

Ugh. I hadn't thought of that. Vee and Kiyoshi would probably go together. Who would I go with? Horrors, horrors.

'Maybe Tariq will ask you,' Fletcher said, slyly.

'Tariq? No way! I mean he's—' I broke off abruptly. I had been about to say that he was gay, but thank God I had stopped myself. I was finally becoming a bit less tactless.

'Were you about to say he's gay?' Fletcher said, psychic-like. 'I promise you he's not.'

'Why do you say that?'

'Because Priscilla was my friend. You get to hear a lot about someone's life when you're jogging together. And I heard all about their relationship.' She rolled her eyes. 'And when I say all about it . . . I mean *all* about it. He is definitely not gay.'

'But that doesn't mean anything,' I said, forgetting the fact that I wasn't meant to be outing him. 'He might have been faking it. Or he might be bi.'

'Maybe. But I promise you, he wasn't faking it.'

'Oh.' I tried to absorb all of this. 'Well, anyway, we're just friends. He's too smooth for me,' I added, to make it sound convincing.

I was so preoccupied, I had barely noticed how much ground we'd covered. We were already back at the entrance to the park. I felt exhausted; my limbs were like spaghetti – but I also felt great. How was this possible?

'You did awesome!' Fletcher said. 'Much better than I even imagined! We ran for fifteen minutes, and then for ten minutes, plus ten minutes walking in between . . . probably about three miles.'

'Three *miles*?' I stared at her, open-mouthed. Impossible. That was an inhuman, Paula Radcliffe-style distance. There was absolutely no way that I could have managed that.

'That's nothing! Next time we'll do five miles. And you know what comes after that?'

'An ice-cream?' I suggested hopefully, nodding towards the stall in the distance.

'An ice-cream for sure. But then . . . 10K, baby.' There was a dangerous gleam in her eyes. 'You and I are entering a race.'

Chapter forty-three

I was so befuddled by everything Fletcher had told me, that I forgot to hide from Mette and Lauren in the communal showers that evening. I just stripped off alongside them, tuning out their talk of where to buy the best slutty underwear in Paris (their words, not mine).

Tariq wasn't gay. His relationship with Priscilla *had* been real. Which meant he must really miss her. And he had obviously just been drunk and lonely up on the roof . . . and now he probably thought that I had a giant crush on him like everyone else in the school. And that I was a pervert who took advantage of drunken boys.

Still: why did he knock on *my* door? *Could* he like me?

No. For a start, Priscilla was an Alpha: beautiful, intelligent, probably going to be running the UN in a few short years. Pretty hard to live up to. Not to mention, he would not want to get involved with anyone so soon after they broke up.

But had there been *something* there? Did I imagine it all?

'Something on your mind, Lola?' Mette asked. 'You look like you're trying to solve quadratic equations.'

'Not really. Just stressing about French homework.' I stepped out and wrapped myself in my towel quickly before they could see my unkempt bikini line – so different from their perfect landing strips. I would have loved their advice, but they were like bloodhounds when it came to gossip; even if I changed all the identities, it would be all around the school before our hair was dry.

I knew Tariq wasn't into me. If he was, he would have kissed me while he had the chance. I didn't know that much about boys, but I knew that there was a difference between a girl who was fun to hang out with, and one that you actually wanted to go out with. I could predict that Tariq would be looking for a trophy girlfriend like Priscilla, and that wasn't me. Not that she was a trophy. More a First Lady.

Feeling sad, I dialled home, but Mum and Dad were out. I tried texting Lenny, but although there was a read receipt, he didn't reply. He was still angry at me; we hadn't spoken in days.

'Sorry,' I texted him. A few minutes later, he sent me an angry face and a poo emoji. So much for me thinking he was growing up too fast.

In the interests of procrastination before homework, I decided to send my dad a quick IM telling him I'd been on a three-mile run. He was a runner too, so that was the kind of thing he'd like to hear. I wasn't sure if it was missing Lenny, or hearing Fletcher say she didn't want to regret things, but a thought had occurred to me. Maybe it was time for *me* to start making an effort with *him*.

To my surprise, I got an IM back from him within minutes. 'Great stuff! Three miles is very decent for the first outing! Make sure you have a pizza or something this evening. Or some pasta. Do they have pasta in France ;)?'

Which was actually the longest message I'd had from him in months. Grinning, I tapped out a few runner emojis in reply and told him that yes, they had pasta in France. I spent a good ten minutes IM-ing back and forth with him before I finally settled down to my homework.

Chapter forty-four

Over the next two days, my suspicions about Tariq proved totally correct. He barely acknowledged me, except for a few awkward waves as we passed each other between classes or at lunch.

It wasn't until Friday afternoon that we finally talked.

I had just come back from another jog with Fletcher, and was at the pigeonhole, seeing if there was any post for me (there never was), when he came up to me.

'Look at you! I didn't know you were so . . . sporty.' He glanced at my Lycra-clad form, then looked away.

'Fletcher made me do it,' I explained.

We both paused as two IB Twos swept by us. As soon as they were out of earshot, he said, going even pinker, 'I am so sorry about the other night, Lola. I was pretty drunk.'

'It's OK. I was half-asleep myself – I can barely remember it.' I almost couldn't look him in the eye, I was so embarrassed. He probably thought I had been cherishing the memory of that night. Which was obviously not the case. Well, not quite.

'All of that stuff I said about the election and every-thing . . . I was being overdramatic. I'm not that bothered about it really. Obviously.'

Oh.

Now I felt even worse. He wasn't worried about the fact he'd put his head in my lap, or that we had almost kissed – or whatever that was. That was insignificant. He *was* embarrassed that he'd revealed his vulnerable feel-ings to me. But his vulnerable feelings weren't about me; they were about the election.

'It's fine,' I said. 'Honestly.'

We walked back into the courtyard where people were sitting under the trees. It was the most beautiful evening – warm and balmy, almost more like summer than spring. And everyone in sight was studying: another clue that exam season was coming. Why was the weather always nicest just before exams? And what on earth was I going to say to him now?

'Lola,' he said. 'Can I ask you a question?'

'Yes, of course,' I said. Suddenly I felt unaccountably shy.

Was he – maybe – going to ask me something personal after all? Maybe even – ask me to the Spring Ball?

Tariq took out a notebook. 'Here's a list of everyone in IB One . . . who I *think* would vote for me. Could you take a look and tell me if you agree?'

'Oh.'

Trying to hide my disappointment, I skimmed over the names. Patrick; Nicolas; Mette; Jun . . . I didn't know them all but it seemed likely enough. He also had Fletcher down; his intelligence must be good.

193

'Yeah, I think you're safe with all these,' I said, eventually.

'What about Kiyoshi? I'm not asking you to talk to him or anything. I just wondered what you thought.'

I tried to put my bruised feelings aside, and look at it objectively.

'Yeah, I think you definitely have Kiyoshi. I can't see him voting for Hunter, anyway.'

'OK, great.' Tariq added the name to his list then paused. 'What about Vee? I know she's maybe not my biggest fan but . . . I can't see her voting for Hunter, can you?'

'No. But I think she might just spoil her ballot or something.'

He nodded. 'And you?' he added, almost shyly.

'Of course you have my vote.'

'Thanks, Lola.' He gave me a quick smile. 'That means a lot. It's just that I keep hearing people saying they're going to vote for Hunter. I have more support among the staff, and in IB One, but the younger kids are really into Hunter . . .'

After a minute or two, I couldn't listen any more.

My last few days had been full of turmoil, wondering what was going on between us. Meanwhile, he was worrying about the election.

I thought I had known him pretty well, but now I saw him so much more clearly than I ever had before. He cared more about random people's opinions and his own popularity rating, than about how I felt. It was nice that he was confiding in me, but it was nothing to do with me. I could have been anyone.

194

As I left him to go in and change, I tried to swallow down my disappointment. I *knew* that it was for the best. Even if he was interested in me – which he wasn't – I could never tell Tariq the truth about myself. No matter what he thought about it personally, it would *look* bad, and to use a reference from my Greek and Roman class, that was his Achilles heel.

Chapter forty-five

Over the next two weeks, the main topics of conversation all over IB One were the election, and the ball. People endlessly discussed what they would dress as, who they would go with, and who they would vote for. I had assumed Tariq would be the firm favourite, but I was hearing more and more people enthusing about Hunter and his pancakes.

Meanwhile, we kept up our running, and I was amazed to find myself actually liking it. On Friday, a week after we'd started, we actually ran five miles. The next day we did a shorter interval training session – polite code for 'hell', but I felt amazing afterwards. For longer runs, our usual route was to run down to Notre Dame, or upriver in the direction of the Invalides bridge with its enormous golden statues. I was seeing more of Paris than I ever had before. I began to look forward to our long runs, and get obsessed with adding another mile or ten more minutes to our time. And with every passing mile, I felt less upset about Tariq.

'You're not going to become one of those running bores, are you – going on about shoes and times and nutrition gels?' said Vee one morning, when I came to breakfast straight from a run.

'No!' I said. I didn't mention that Dad had given me some advice about running shoes via IM that morning, and I was planning to get new ones in a shop where they analysed your gait.

'But we are doing a race,' I added, proudly. 'Me and Fletcher.'

'You and Fletcher,' said Vee. 'That sounds so *super fun*. Are you going to be BFFs?'

'Well, she is my friend,' I said, uneasily. 'I'm allowed to have other friends, aren't I?'

I realised that I felt uncomfortable even saying this, which was ridiculous. What were we, thirteen?

'Yes – of course you are,' Vee muttered. 'Sorry.'

Later, Kiyoshi said that Vee was under a lot of stress these days with her parents, and not to take her too seriously.

'She always feels a bit threatened by her friends getting new friends. I think it's because her parents moved around so much when she was small. She hates change. No, not like that! Like this.'

We were in the same sushi restaurant we'd been to when I first arrived, having an early dinner. Kiyoshi had insisted I had to learn to use chopsticks.

I wanted to be understanding about Vee, but really, she was becoming exhausting – far more exhausting, in her own way, than a five-mile run. I couldn't believe how sophisticated and cool she had seemed when I first met her. Now I thought she was like an angry five-year-old. I even felt bad for having dinner with Kiyoshi without her, though she was at the ballet with her mother.

In any case, I had enough on my mind with school work, the awkwardness with Tariq – and the problem of what to wear to the ball, and more importantly, who to go with. Kiyoshi was going with Vee, or he would have asked me.

'You didn't want to ask Marco?'

'No way!' said Kiyoshi.

'Is he still with the messaging?'

'He is still with the messaging.' He sighed. 'This is one of the many reasons it sucks to be gay. Because as well as not working out if someone likes you, you have to work out if they're the right orientation. And my gaydar is obviously all wrong, judging by Tariq.'

I had told Kiyoshi earlier about Tariq; all he had said was, 'I still think he's hiding *something*.'

'I was just thinking,' he continued. 'Have you noticed that it's always the people whose parents are divorced who have the best love lives? Hunter's parents are divorced . . . And so are Tyger's . . . They're always in relationships.'

'What's your parents' marriage like?'

'Made in heaven.'

We both laughed.

'I don't think it's your parents,' I said. 'Honestly, maybe you just need to take a risk with Marco.' I paused. 'Don't take this the wrong way. But do you actually want things to happen with Marco? Or is there maybe a part of you that feels safer having it all just be messages?'

'Ouch,' he said. 'You know . . . I think you may be right.'

'Really?' I asked.

'Really. But I do want to try,' he continued.

'Maybe, instead of making a move in real life, you could send him a flirty message,' I suggested. 'Like . . . say you can't wait to see him in his outfit at the ball.'

He looked thoughtful. 'That's not a bad idea,' he said.

'Do it! I mean, why wouldn't he like you? You're lovely and talented . . .'

Kiyoshi seemed to cheer up. 'You think so? Hey, maybe you're right.'

'Of course I am.'

Our food arrived just then to distract us from our love-in. I started wolfing down my vegetarian set. How had I ever found chopsticks hard? They were easy now.

Kiyoshi pushed some of his sushi towards me. 'Have a tiny bit of this salmon one. Just to try.'

'Oh, I don't know . . .'

'Come on Lola. You have to try some sushi! If I can send a flirty message to a boy I like, you can try sushi.'

I felt duty-bound not to be wimp, so I grabbed it awkwardly with my chopsticks.

'Just forget that it's fish. Think of it as a new thing. It actually doesn't taste of fish at all.'

I obeyed him, cautiously sinking my teeth into the piece of sushi. To my amazement, he was totally right. It tasted bland and cool and refreshing, especially with the salty soy and the spicy wasabi.

'This is actually really delicious!' I said. 'Can I have another one?' I tried a tuna roll, a prawn sushi roll, and a delicious one with mackerel. I ate so much, in fact, that I had to order more. And with every bite, I was getting more and more adept with my chopsticks.

'I can't believe it. I like sushi!' I said.

I took a photo of my sushi and sent it to Dad quickly. Within minutes, I got a thumbs-up emoji back. I smiled. Why had this never occurred to me before? Dad was terrible on the phone, but he gave great text.

'You've transformed me into a sushi lover! I feel so sophisticated. Next, I'm going to start liking jazz, and modern art. And whisky!'

Kiyoshi shook his head. 'No, I didn't. It was all you. It's like they say: you can't change people, but people can change.'

'I really like that! Who said that?'

He looked pleased with himself. 'I did.'

Chapter forty-six

It was still early when I got back – not quite eight. Fletcher's door was open; she was lying on her bed reading a magazine.

'Lola!' she said, when she saw me. 'Can I ask you something?' She rolled over and held up her magazine. 'Am I a Basic Becky?'

'*What?*'

She read aloud: '*The BB carries a Michael Kors bag in one hand and a skinny latte in the other. She drinks white wine, vodka and soda, and goes crazy for Pumpkin Spice Latte. She wears fit-flops in summer and Uggs in winter. She's not a natural blonde, but she would die rather than let her roots show. She is really into either soul cycle, glow yoga or Pilates, and she will never, ever do anything that will surprise you.*'

I leaned against her door frame, not sure what to say.

'No of course not! For a start, your name's Fletcher, not Becky.'

'But I do *all* of those things,' she said, wide-eyed.

The truth was, that *did* sound like Fletcher in lots of ways – not least because this seemed to be the first time she'd heard the expression. I'd never seen her really even use the internet aside from Instagram – she seemed to get all of her information from out-of-date magazines, like this one.

'Look,' I tried. 'That's a really stupid, sexist expression. Misogynist, even. I mean, there's no male equivalent, is there?'

She looked back at the list. '*Her style icon is Kate Middleton,*' she read. '*My* style icon is Kate Middleton!'

'Fletcher, there's nothing wrong with being mainstream,' I said. 'Who cares if you like Pumpkin Spice Latte? It's nice! You should just like what you like.' I paused, as I thought about how I could do with taking that advice.

'And anyway, they're totally wrong about you never doing anything to surprise anyone.'

'How do you mean?'

'Well, you dumped Hunter. That was sassy.'

'Maybe. But I still feel like the whole school is laughing at me.'

'They're not, at *all*. They're laughing at him. Him and his stupid pancakes.'

'Thanks, Lola.' She brightened. 'Actually something nice did happen today.'

'Oh, what?' I came over and sat on the end of her bed.

'Tariq asked me to the ball. Wasn't that sweet of him?'

Her happy expression felt like a blow to my stomach. My throat suddenly felt as though it was closing up. I managed to say, 'Very sweet.'

'I think he knew I was dreading going by myself. It's not a romantic thing, obviously, but it's so nice not to have to go alone.' She gave a little frown. 'You don't mind, do you?'

'Of course not! We are just friends. Like I said.' I tried to smile.

'But even if you are just friends – you might have wanted to ask him . . .'

'No, *honestly*.' How many times would I have to lie about this?

'But who will you go with?'

'I'll dig someone up.' My smile became a rictus grin. 'Listen, I've got to do my homework. I'll see you tomorrow. And don't worry about the stupid magazine!'

Chapter forty-seven

Needless to say, I didn't get much homework done.

After barely five minutes at my desk, I got up, put my hoody on over my jeans and T-shirt, and left the building. It was warm enough, for the first time, to go out without a jacket in the evening. I walked down the rue de Vaugirard, with its cafés teeming with people sitting outside, which always reminded me of the Van Gogh painting 'Starry Night'. Then I wandered down place Saint Sulpice. The big fountain in the middle, with its stone lions, looked more magical than ever, the water illuminated by floodlights in the spring dusk. Everything was beautiful. Everything was awful.

The loveliness of the spring evening couldn't distract me from Tariq and Fletcher. No wonder Tariq had asked her. She was tall and blonde and beautiful – not to mention sweet and kind and bright. They would look great in photographs. Maybe he was even planning on asking her out. Why wouldn't he? Miserably restless, I started walking back towards the school.

Soon I was at the sports block, which was in an annexe

a few doors down from the main building. I had never even known of its existence until a week or two ago, which said a lot about my lifestyle.

I slipped in, looking for distractions. Maybe I would even go to the gym? Not something I'd ever have contemplated before. But I had a lot more energy now that I was running.

The sports annexe was like a smaller version of our building, built around the same courtyard plan. At the far end of the courtyard was a low window where you could see into the basement where the the fencing court was. There was a light on, and I came closer to see.

A pair of boys were sparring, while the rest watched. With their white uniforms and black masks, they looked like something from a costume drama.

The taller one was obviously winning. He seemed to be a step ahead of his opponent at all times, stabbing with his long blade. Then the second guy seemed to rally, pushing back. I'd never thought fencing was easy, but as I watched them lunge back and forth, arms reaching and thighs straining, I realised just how hard it must be.

There was something about this display of masculine aggression that was very, well, sexy. I didn't even know these guys but you could tell how strong they were. And fit.

Just then, the shorter boy ducked to avoid the taller one's blade, and swung in with a sneaky counter-attack. But the taller one swung away from the blow and came back with one of his own, pinning his sword right to the centre of his opponent's chest. The electric sensors buzzed.

'*Touché*,' said the smaller one, holding up his hand.

They drew off their black masks, and saluted, before pulling off a glove each for a left-handed handshake. As the taller one turned round, I felt a shock that wasn't a total shock. Because I had known, on some level, that it was Tariq.

He looked up, and I stepped back quickly into the darkness, before he could see me.

It was as if I'd seen him getting out of the shower or something. Though that would actually be less disturbing than the way he looked right now – hair flattened with sweat, dark face flushed against his white vest. Basically, a picture I would be unable to forget any time soon.

One of his fencing-mates – one of the girls – was helping unzip the back of his vest. His T-shirt, underneath, was also soaked with sweat. For the second time today, I was shot through with jealousy.

I turned round and started walking, feeling my misery multiply with every step.

How could I have been so stupid? To fall for someone so far out of my league, without even realising I was doing it. To think that we were just friends, when actually I had a giant, painful crush on him, which was probably visible to the eye, like the Ready Brek glow. I doubted I would ever be able to look him in the eye again.

My heart sank even further as I realised how much I would miss him. He was my best friend here – or he had been. Fletcher and Kiyoshi were great, and I still liked Vee – with reservations – but Tariq was the person I would miss the most. But I had caught feelings for him. Which meant that we could never be friends again the way we used to be.

'The gym's about to close, you know.'

It was one of the teaching assistants. I hurried off to bed, hoping not to bump into Tariq, or anyone else, on the way.

Chapter forty-eight

It was fairly easy to avoid Tariq for the rest of the week. As exam season was approaching, everyone was starting to spend more and more time in their rooms or in the library, fuelled by endless coffees and junk food. I was under much less pressure because I was only doing the certificate. So I had extra time to brood, and also to agonise over my outfit for the ball. I knew I wanted to wear black, with a veil – but I didn't want to look like a Gothic Miss Havisham. I was gloomy enough as it was. And also, even though I knew Tariq wouldn't be looking at me, I really wanted him to see me at my best. Whatever that was.

'I just get really confused about clothes in general,' I said to Fletcher one day, when we were sitting in my room studying. 'I never know whether I want to look classic, or edgy, or rock chick or cute, or what.' I held up my ripped jeans and my trench coat.

'Can't you be both?' Fletcher said.

'How do you mean?'

'Well, one day you could wear something edgy. And another day you could dress as preppy girl. Depending on how you feel.' She beamed. 'And you could combine them. I mean, those jeans would go great with that trench. And your Great Catsby sweater . . . Which I love, by the way . . . Couldn't you wear that with your little suede skirt?'

I stared at all the items she mentioned, my head practically spinning.

'Fletcher,' I said, 'you're a genius.'

To test her theory, I whipped on my ripped jeans with my polo neck, and stepped into my high heels. 'No, that looks weird, though.'

She narrowed her eyes. 'I think the polo neck is fighting with the heels.'

'Yes! Let me try with my ankle boots instead.'

That worked perfectly. So did the heels with one of my slogan T-shirts.

'I can't believe I've never thought of that before,' I admitted. I sat down. 'This sounds crazy, but I feel like I've been wearing different clothes almost based on who I'm with, instead of what I want.'

'Unless you're meeting the Pope, that doesn't make sense,' she agreed.

'Do you ever feel like you're a different person depending on who you're talking to?' I said. 'I sometimes feel like my friends come from such different worlds, it means I'm leading a double life. Or a triple one.'

Fletcher considered this. 'I don't think that's a bad thing, though,' she said. 'The fact that you have different types of friends doesn't mean there's anything wrong with you. It shows that your personality has lots of different facets, which is good. I feel like my friends and I used to all dress the same and act the same. And that wasn't great either.' She made a face. 'That reminds me . . . Have you heard? Hunter is furious that Tariq's asked me to the ball. Apparently he said to Riley, "This means war".'

'Ugh,' I tried to say sympathetically. Though it was hard to sympathise with the problem of two men fighting over you, when I couldn't even stay friends with one. Looking on the bright side: if Tariq and I weren't friends any more, that was one less alternative life to worry about.

Chapter forty-nine

'Turn around,' said Fletcher.

Kiyoshi turned around slowly, revealing his outfit; a sharp white suit, shirt and tie.

'It is uh-*may*-zing,' said Fletcher. 'Honestly Kiyoshi, you look like a hot Disney prince.'

'Really? Thanks,' he said, with a smile, smoothing his hair back and looking at himself critically. 'I do like this suit.'

It was finally Saturday; the day of the ball, and we were in Fletcher's room getting ready. I had bought a simple black dress from the supermarket Monoprix, and Kiyoshi had unearthed a fabulous waterfall of a black lace veil with scalloped edges. I'd never put on a veil before and I had to say, it did make a person look fairly mysterious and magical. We had all taken turns trying it on, even Kiyoshi. But I felt sad as I thought that, no matter how good I looked, it would make no difference to Tariq. He would be along to pick Fletcher up shortly. I had to be gone by then.

'It looks perfect with your hair,' said Fletcher.

'Do you think?' I patted my hair cautiously. The night before, I had dyed it back to my original dark brown. It was a scary step but I felt happy about it. I was finally feeling a bit more like myself. Or rather, I finally felt that I knew who that was.

'You look like a Sicilian widow on the way to a Mafioso funeral,' Kiyoshi was saying.

'Oh no,' I said suddenly. 'You don't think that it's going to be, like, triggering? Or that I'm being insensitive to people who've lost loved ones . . .'

Kiyoshi and Fletcher stared at me blankly.

'Nobody is going to think that,' said Kiyoshi. 'Now, what do I do with my hair? Product or no product?'

'No product!' Fletcher said. 'You have such great hair, it doesn't need anything.'

To my great surprise, Fletcher and Kiyoshi had become pretty friendly over the couple of weeks. She had already heard all about the Marco Agnelli situation and advised being cool, not replying to all his messages, and letting him make the first move. Kiyoshi, in turn, had been helping her with her maths homework and also her costume, though she had refused his suggestion of a rubber Black Widow-type costume.

'I just assumed she would be homophobic,' he admitted to me. 'Which makes an ass out of me and me.'

'Where's Vee?' I asked Kiyoshi, as he finished his winged eyeliner. 'I haven't seen her in days. She hasn't replied to my texts either.'

'Oh, she's with Priya I think. I asked her if she wanted to get ready with us and she said no.' He shrugged.

'Is she still planning on wearing her US flag?' Fletcher asked. Vee had been planning to wrap herself in an enormous Stars and Stripes to depict the Triumph of Imperialist Capitalism.

'I think so,' said Kiyoshi, looking worried. 'I really really hope it doesn't cause a fight.'

Then, of course, there were the obligatory selfies. I was worried about them going on Instagram but at least I had a big heavy veil. If only I could wear it all the time.

'When is your date picking you up?' Kiyoshi asked me, grinning.

'Don't,' I said.

The day before, I had received an invitation from Richard – the *Star Trek* fan in the year below us. I didn't have the heart to say no.

Fletcher said reassuringly, 'Honestly, Lola, everybody will know that you're just being kind by going with him. That's if anybody notices at all.'

I nodded sadly. That was how it looked to Fletcher, because she was so nice, but the world would judge it differently. She was also probably the only girl in the school who had resisted the urge to get sexy in her costume – instead wearing brown leggings, a suede waistcoat and a white shirt, and a toy bow and arrow over her shoulder.

'That's Tariq,' she said, checking her phone. 'He's going to come over. He says he's even got a corsage for me!'

'A what? Where did he even get one?' said Kiyoshi. 'A museum?'

'Cool!' I said. 'Oh, sorry. I just remembered I have to do a thing though – I have to, um, call my parents. I'll see you both at the Ball, OK?'

Kiyoshi called after me, 'Don't get so busy making out with Richard that you forget the ball is on. I know what you crazy kids are like!'

I bolted back to my room, to the sound of their merry laughter.

Chapter fifty

It was reassuring in a way that, even though Jean Monnet was so sophisticated, the Ball was still a school ball like any other, in the same hall where we had assembly. There were the white lights – installed under Fletcher's supervision by the school's grumpy caretaker after much signing of forms. There was a long table with punch, plastic cups, and a modest amount of beers and the controversial snacks. It wasn't quite a magical fairyland, but it looked very pretty.

Rose, in a plunging, feathery pink dress, clearly didn't care that Fletcher had got her way on snacks. Priya, in a dress covered in hearts, was waltzing around with Tyger, who was dressed as, well, a tiger. No surprises there.

'Hello, Lola.'

It was Vee. Contrary to what she'd said, she was wearing a very severe Greek-style dress that set her olive skin off perfectly. Her hair was caught up on top of her head, and she wore a crown of green leaves. Of course; she was the Greek goddess Victory. I had never seen her look so stunning.

'You look fantastic, Vee,' I said sincerely. 'Where've you been? I feel like I haven't seen you in ages.'

'Here and there,' she smiled. 'What are you meant to be exactly?'

'Sorrow,' I explained. 'Lola is short for Dolores which means Sorrow. Bit of a weird one, but there it is.'

'Yeah, it is weird,' she said, musingly. 'Especially because . . .'

She paused weirdly, making me feel nervous.

'Never mind,' she said brightly, after a minute. 'Enjoy the party.' And she was gone.

I had no time to speculate about what that was all about, because Richard was back with two paper cups full of beer.

'Thanks!' I put back my veil, and necked mine gratefully. It had to be said, Richard was being a pretty good date so far. To get me beer was thoughtful. *Positive thinking*, I told myself.

'It should be Romulan ale, shouldn't it!' he said.

'Yes,' I said weakly.

Richard, of course, was wearing a *Star Trek* outfit. A full, mustard-coloured Captain Kirk uniform. I *knew* this would happen. I was fairly certain that he would have worn this even to the original Venetian Ball.

'Doesn't your name mean "king"?' I asked him. I had googled this to make sure I knew what to expect in terms of his costume.

But Richard was ready for me. 'Aha. You see, I'm actually dressed as Captain Kirk in Season One, Episode Fourteen, which of course is called . . .'

I shook my head.

'*The Conscience of the King*! Get it? It's the one where Kirk is sent to Planet Q, to investigate this guy who's pretending to be an actor putting on Hamlet, but he's actually a mass murderer. At least, Kirk is originally sent there to investigate this new food source . . .'

I looked around the room. I had just seen Tariq come in, with Fletcher. He was wearing . . . football gear? Oh, of course. His name meant 'Striker'. I just so happened to have googled that, too. He and Fletcher were talking to Nicolas and Rose, and they all looked like they were having a fabulous time.

'Of course,' Richard was saying, 'I could also have dressed as King Abdullah of Jordan. He actually appeared in an episode in Season Two. That's *Star Trek: The Next Generation* obviously. I can't remember the episode number. Let me see. I can google it . . .'

'No, it's fine,' I said quickly.

The next hour crawled by. I talked to Richard's computer-nerdy friends. Kiyoshi and Marco Agnelli seemed to be getting on great. Tariq and Fletcher were everywhere to be seen, though I avoided them as much as possible. Hunter caused a stir by appearing in full army camouflage, with a fake gun that the teachers immediately took away from him. American Ben, one of Richard's friends, horrified me by saying he wanted to vote for him.

'I really like pancakes,' was all he could say.

'Hi,' said a voice behind us.

It was Tariq, in his blue football shorts and blue-and-white strip. I tried not to stare at his legs.

'You look nice, Lola.' His gaze travelled up to my hair, and he smiled. 'I miss the pink, though.'

'Does Tariq mean footballer?' Richard asked, frowning.

'No, it means striker,' I said without thinking. 'Or morning star.'

Tariq stared at me. Your friendly neighbourhood stalker.

'I googled everybody's names,' I muttered, turning scarlet. 'Just to make sure I knew, um, what to expect.'

Tariq suddenly said, 'That reminds me. Lola, can I just grab you for a minute? I mean, borrow you. I wanted to look over those prizes with you. Is that OK, Richard?'

'There are prizes?' Richard said, brightening. 'Cool. I'll be with these guys.'

Tariq led me out of the room, and to a nearby stair-case. I had never seen it before but it led up to the balcony that overlooked the hall. Yet another hidden nook in this school.

It was fun to look down on the whole room full of costumed people, dancing and talking. It would be the perfect place to make an announcement, or just really freak people out *Carrie*-style.

'What about the prizes?' I asked him.

He leaned against the balcony railing. 'I don't want to talk to you about prizes. I just came up here so we wouldn't be disturbed.'

'Oh.' My heart started to pound. Either he had taken me here to kill me, or he was annoyed with me, or . . .

'Are you here with Richard? Like, on a date?' He didn't meet my eye as he said this.

'With *Richard*? No,' I said. 'He asked me, and I didn't want to be rude.'

'But you were talking about someone who kept messaging you, and you didn't know what it meant . . .'

'That was happening to someone else! I told you!' I looked at him wildly. 'Are you here with Fletcher as a date?'

He shook his head.

'That night on the roof,' he said, still looking down. 'I wanted something to happen, but I didn't have the nerve. I didn't want to lose you as a friend.'

My hopes were rising and falling like a rollercoaster. He continued, 'But now I don't care. I don't just want you as a friend. I mean, I do. But seeing you tonight, looking like that, with another guy . . . it made me realise I want more.'

I was shaken and flooded, from head to toe, with such a torrent of emotions, I couldn't even form a single word. It was like a dream. Tariq *wanted* me.

It was time to admit it. I wanted him more than any boy I'd ever met. And it wasn't just physical; he was my friend, too – my best friend.

'Tariq, I . . .'

'It's fine, if you don't feel the same,' he said, in a voice I hardly recognised.

'I do,' I managed to say. 'I *do* feel the same. I just have to tell you something first.'

'What?'

I wished that I could throw myself into his arms. But I couldn't – not yet. It was suddenly very important that I not kiss him until he knew the truth about me.

'Can I tell you another time?' I said finally. 'It would take too long now. Fletcher will be waiting for you. And Richard's waiting for me . . .'

He smiled. 'OK.'

I turned round to walk downstairs, but he grabbed my hand.

'Wait,' he said in a hoarse voice. And then he kissed me.

Chapter fifty-one

I. Have. Never.

Hadakisslikethatinmyentire *life*.

It was the kiss to end all kisses. I couldn't move or speak; I could barely breathe. And judging by his face, he felt the same.

'Lola,' he said. Then, 'Shh. What's that?'

There were footsteps on the stairs behind us. With incredible presence of mind, Tariq took a step backwards while I whipped my veil back on.

'Oh, there you are, Tariq,' said Rose. 'We need to do the prizes, are you ready?'

'Sure – we were just taking photos,' said Tariq. Once again, I marvelled at his unbelievable ability to think on his feet. Though anyone less self-absorbed than Rose would have seen straight through this, judging from our guilty expressions.

We all walked downstairs together. Tariq and I studiously avoided each others' gazes except to look at each other, once – and grin at each other stupidly.

As we rejoined the others, the temptation was really strong to stand next to him – maybe let my arm brush against his, or even put my hand in his. But I couldn't do that to Fletcher, or Richard; it would be really rude. Giving Tariq one last look, I went off to find Richard, and apologise for taking so long.

'That's OK!' he said. 'We've been talking about Settlers of Catan. Have you ever played?'

I shook my head. At that moment, I spotted Kiyoshi leaving the room, grinning very widely, and walking very close to Marco Agnelli.

'Oh my God!'

'What is it?'

I recovered myself. 'Nothing,' I said, feeling relieved. I had actually managed to stop myself from blurting something out tactlessly. Things were looking up on all fronts.

'Hi everyone!' Rose was saying into the microphone. 'Welcome to our Spring Ball!'

As she went on – giving the speech that I thought Fletcher should really have been delivering – I looked nervously, sideways, at Tariq's handsome profile across the room. I still didn't know how to tell him. But I felt more hopeful now. He did really like me. He would understand.

'And now it's time to give the prizes for best costume!' Rose was saying. 'Third prize goes to . . . Abigail Wu!'

Abigail shrieked and ran up the steps to collect her prize. She was wearing an old-fashioned maid's uniform with a white skirt and frilly cap. Abigail obviously meant maid.

'Second prize . . . Jason Deslandes! Jason, what does your costume mean?'

'Jason means healer,' said Jason, who was dressed as a doctor.

'And in first place – Vee Collins!'

'Woohoo! Go Vee!' I joined in the applause, thrilled for Vee. Her costume *was* fantastic. As she took her place on the stage, I found myself hoping that a bit of recognition would help stop her feeling so angry with everything.

'Thanks,' she said into the microphone. 'I just want to say a quick word while I'm here – firstly to thank everyone for organising the party . . .'

I was quite surprised; that was very nice of her.

'And secondly, I want to make everyone aware of something.'

I smiled to myself, thinking: this was much more like Vee. She was obviously channelling all those actors who made political speeches at the Oscars.

'There should really be a prize tonight . . .' She paused, and looked directly into my eyes, 'for the most complete disguise. There's someone here who's been in disguise for months. Ever since she got here.'

My hands went icy cold. I swallowed.

'We know her as Lola, but that's not her name. Her name is Delilah Hoover. She got kicked out of her school, for being racist—'

That was as far as she got before a teacher pulled her away from the microphone. Vee instantly started writhing around, making it look as if he was dragging her forcibly. Talking fast, she yelled, 'I've linked to her real name on our page. She's not who she says she is!'

223

Something seemed to happen to my balance, and I wobbled. Richard grabbed me. Everyone around me was staring at me, and whispering. I saw Priya take out her phone and look at it, then at me.

Fletcher came flying over to me.

'Lola, what is she talking about? She's crazy, right?'

All I could do was shake my head, and then hurry out of the hall as fast as my legs could take me. I left so fast, I didn't even see Tariq's reaction.

Chapter fifty-two

Back in my room. Curled up on my bed. This felt so familiar.

She's not who she says she is.

She got kicked out of her school for being racist.

I couldn't believe that Vee had done that, but on the other hand, of course I could. In any case, it was done now. Everybody knew.

I found myself actually wriggling around, writhing like a worm under a spade, trying to escape it. But there was no getting away this time. I pictured them all talking about me, sharing and tweeting the story. It was happening all over again. And it would be worse this time, because of the fact that I'd lied about it.

I checked our class Facebook page. Vee had linked to the BBC article, which reproduced the original tweet. There were already two comments under it.

That is so horrible! No wonder she lied.

OMG I can't believe someone would say that.

They were from people I didn't know very well. Vee hadn't written anything else, and nor had Fletcher or

Kiyoshi. I wondered what they were thinking. What Tariq was thinking. He would probably never speak to me again.

I almost admired Vee for doing it openly like that. She could so easily have just posted it online, anonymously. But she did it in public. And she gave me a chance to tell her the truth – which I turned down.

The true horror of my situation was beginning to dawn on me. At least when things went bad at my old school, I could go home and be safe there. But now I had landed myself in a place where it was all school, all the time.

I rolled over and FaceTimed Mum.

'Finally!' she said, which made me feel really guilty. 'We haven't heard from you in so long!'

'Mum . . .' But I couldn't get the words out. As soon as I heard her voice, the tears started to come.

Mum started freaking out at the other end of the line. 'Delilah! What is it? What's happened?'

But she must have known, even before I managed to gasp, 'They found out.'

'I'm so sorry, love,' she said.

I gulped and hiccupped, while she just stayed quiet on the other end.

'I have to leave,' I managed to say, eventually.

'Slow down. When did this happen?'

'Just now. It was at the Spring Ball.' I glanced at myself in the top corner of the screen. With my tear-streaked face under my black veil, my Sorrow costume was a lot more appropriate now.

'Well, at least . . .'

I tensed up, not feeling in the mood for one of Mum's positive spins on things.

'At least now that it's out in the open, you can give them all your side of the story.'

I stared at her in disbelief. 'What? Mum! They are never going to listen to me. I've lied to them all.'

'Well . . .' she hesitated. 'The thing is, love – it was always going to come out sooner or later. Don't you think?'

'No, I don't think! That's easy for you to say – you don't have to stay here and face everyone . . . I can't do it. I can't do this *all over again*.' I was choked with sobs.

'Oh, love . . . Of course you can come home,' Mum said, once I'd subsided. 'You know you can always come home.'

'When?' I sobbed.

Mum wanted me to wait until after the exams; I wanted to leave for the Eurostar then and there. In the end we compromised; I could come home in a week.

'Just let me wait forty-eight hours before I book the train. OK? The people there might surprise you.'

'I doubt it,' I said.

Chapter fifty-three

Once I'd got off the phone with Mum, I turned my phone onto airplane mode, closed my laptop, and plugged myself into some music. I felt a bit like Schrodinger's cat – the one who could be alive or dead depending on what had happened inside the box. I was fine, as long as I didn't leave my box.

Then there was a knock at the door. I was almost too scared to open it, but there was always the chance that it might be Tariq.

'Who is it?'

'It's me!'

Fletcher, still in her costume. She reached out and hugged me, while I stood there in shock.

'I just wish you would've told me!' she said.

Had told me, I thought irrelevantly.

'I didn't think you would believe me.'

Fletcher sat down. 'Just tell me everything that happened.'

So I told her the whole thing. Getting obsessed with the Twitter feed of Dream Uni; trying to impress them with my witty tweets; the technology Sabbath – and then the aftermath. Pleading with my parents to let me come to Jean Monnet.

'But didn't your friends believe you? Didn't they understand?'

'They said they believed me. But . . . I don't know. I just couldn't talk to them any more. Maybe if we'd been better friends, it wouldn't have mattered.'

'I know what you mean,' Fletcher said. 'That's basically what happened with me and Riley and August.'

'How do you mean?'

'I'm not comparing the two things, at all. I'm just trying to say, I know what it's like to walk into the dining hall and feeling like everyone's staring at you. And you must have noticed, I'm not friends with Riley or August any more. So I know what it's like to feel alone.'

'But you didn't do anything wrong.'

'Neither did you!' said Fletcher. 'Anyone looking at that tweet can tell you were trying to be sarcastic. It's just not even a thing.'

The relief, from hearing her say that, was overwhelming. But was it just a coincidence that the only other person to think it was NBD just happened to be a white girl like me?

'So what are you going to do now?' Fletcher said.

'I'm leaving.'

'Leaving?'

'Yeah. I've spoken to my mum – she said I could come home. I have to have a cool-down period of forty-eight hours, but then she'll book me a Eurostar home.'

'But you can't leave! What about your exams? And, what about the race?'

'My exams don't really matter so much. I'm only doing the IB certificate, after all. And I'm sorry about the race, but . . .'

She didn't say anything but she didn't have to. Fletcher's face was always worth a thousand words.

'But what happens after you get home? Do you go back to your old school? Or do you find a new school and make up another name? You can't keep running forever.'

So everyone kept telling me.

'I don't know,' I said, my eyes brimming again. 'I just know I can't stay here.'

'Yes, you can,' said Fletcher. 'I mean – you might not *want* to, but you can.'

'But—'

'How do you think I felt?' she said. 'I mean I know it's not quite as bad, but . . . believe me; after the Hunter thing, I didn't want to stay here either.'

I couldn't think of anything to say to that.

'Sleep on it,' Fletcher said. 'But listen – whatever happens, I've got your back. OK?'

'Don't. You'll make me cry again.' I hugged her, thinking how lucky I was to have a friend like her and how little I deserved it. It almost – almost – made up for the fact that I still hadn't heard anything from Tariq yet.

Chapter fifty-four

I didn't sleep at all that night.

At five a.m. I got up and started packing.

By eight a.m., I was packed and I'd formulated a plan. I would just stay here, in my room, until my cool-down period had passed and I could get my train. I had some Pringles and Haribo stashed away. Fletcher could smuggle me more food, and I would wait here until it was time for my train. Simple.

I was just beginning to wonder if I could get Mum to shorten the deadline, when there was a knock on the door. It was Ms Curtis, and Mr Gerardo.

'We brought you breakfast,' said Mr Gerardo, holding out a paper plate with croissants on it, from the cafeteria. And a banana. Which seemed incongruous and a bit poignant.

'Fletcher's filled us in on what happened. And we've spoken to your parents.' Ms Curtis looked around, noting my suddenly empty room. 'Can we sit down?'

'Look, Lola. We don't think this is a crime,' said Mr Gerardo. He smiled sadly. 'I see now why you wrote so eloquently about a shame culture. But the thing about shame is that it doesn't always come from an actual crime, does it? Sometimes it's just a way of making people feel better, when things are confusing, by displacing "bad" things onto a convenient scapegoat.'

That was all very well, but it didn't help if you were the one tied up outside the village, waiting for the lions to get you.

Mr Gerardo said, 'It's clear that you didn't mean what you said. It was just a mistake.'

'You didn't use your best judgement, maybe,' Ms Curtis added. 'But you intended to be . . . the opposite of racist. Am I right?'

'Yes. But that still doesn't make it OK.'

'I have a suggestion,' Ms Curtis said. 'What about explaining your side of the story? At a community meeting?'

'In front of everyone?' I started to panic again. 'No, I can't. I mean I couldn't.'

The two teachers looked at each other. 'We've removed the article from the Facebook page,' Ms Curtis said. 'And we've sent an email reminding everyone of our anti-bullying policy. You won't have any problems. If you do, come to us or any of the staff.'

I couldn't believe how good they were being about all this. So much better than my old teachers, who just didn't want to deal with it. Maybe it would actually be OK? Maybe people would understand that I wasn't being completely evil?

'OK. I'll try. I mean, I'll try to stay and go to class and stuff.'

'Attagirl,' said Fletcher, appearing behind them. 'Look – you know I've got a geography trip today? We're going to Chartres.'

'What? No, I didn't.' Panic came back to me.

'You'll be fine,' she assured me.

'Fletcher's right,' said Ms Curtis. 'Come on. Let's get you to class.'

Chapter fifty-five

If I thought something super-dramatic was going to happen I was wrong. It was a totally normal morning of classes. Jun surprised us all, in French, by knowing the past conditional perfectly. Mr Woods, the English teacher, explained to us how Shakespeare was the Jay-Z of his day.

But there were little things. People giving me odd looks. Priya rushing away when I came over, though she might just have been late for chemistry. In the breaks between classes, people seemed to melt away when I approached. I saw Kiyoshi in the distance once, but he was deep in conversation with Marco Agnelli. He gave me an awkward wave, then looked away. I tried not to mind.

At lunch time, I went out to a café off campus, where I ate a sad and solitary crepe. I was crossing the court-yard, on my way to class, when I ran into Vee.

I was tempted to slink away but she stood her ground. Well, if she could do that so could I.

'Why did you do it?' I asked, once she got close enough to hear me.

'Me? Why did *you* do it? You told me you changed your name because you got death threats for being a feminist. And I believed you. Like a retard.'

Now wasn't the time to call Vee out for her un-PC language.

'I shouldn't have done that. But I was scared. I didn't think you would understand, if I told you the truth.'

'Understand what – that you got kicked out of your last school for being racist?'

'But I wasn't,' I protested. 'I was trying to make a joke – a stupid joke.'

'That's what all racists say.'

'But it's true!'

Vee shook her head. 'I thought we were friends,' she said. 'I told you things about myself – real things – but you just lied to me.'

Of all the things she'd said, that one hit home the most.

'God knows what else you've done. This is probably just the tip of the iceberg!' she continued.

'Fine. If you want to know, I didn't tell you because I knew you would be judgemental and nutty about it – like you are about everything.'

The next thing I knew, Vee had lashed out at me. When I lifted my face from my covered hands, I saw that someone had grabbed her – Tariq. There were no teachers around, so it was lucky he had.

'Vee!' Kiyoshi rushed forward. 'Come on. This isn't helping.' He put an arm around her and led her away, shooting a reproachful look – not at her, but at *me*. In ordinary circumstances that would have really upset me but I didn't have time to worry about Kiyoshi; I was too busy getting up the courage to face Tariq.

'Thanks,' I mumbled. I looked up and saw an expression on his face that I had never seen before. He looked as though he didn't know me.

Tariq glanced around at all the people watching us. 'OK, guys, this isn't street theatre – please get to class,' he said loudly, and they walked away.

He released my shoulders gently – only then did I realise that he'd been holding them.

'Tariq,' I said. 'You believe me, don't you? I mean – you know I didn't mean it . . . I mean I meant it as a joke . . .'

'I don't know what to think,' he said.

My words tumbling over each other, I tried to explain as best I could. But he didn't seem to be listening.

'It's time for class. Will you be OK?' he asked, distantly.

'Yes. Sure. I'll be fine.'

'Good,' he said.

'Tariq—' I said, but he was gone.

Chapter fifty-six

The day went downhill from there. Now I definitely wasn't imagining it; everyone *was* talking about me. They were way too civilised to *say* anything – this was Jean Monnet, after all. But I could feel the stares directed at my back.

Only six more hours, I thought. *Only six more hours and Mum will book my train home.*

Obviously, I skipped dinner in the cafeteria and ate Pringles in my room instead. I was getting really sick of Pringles. Nobody came round. Not even Tariq. Especially not Tariq.

I shut my eyes and replayed his kiss and his words. *I want more.* That was what he said. It was the perfect thing, until it wasn't.

Of course he was angry. Not just because of what I did, but the fact that I lied about it. I had had months and months to tell him, and I didn't. Now I couldn't blame him for hating me. Some things you just couldn't explain.

Chapter fifty-seven

I was lying in bed the next morning, after another sleepless night, when there was the hammer of a fist at my door. It was Fletcher, back from her geography trip and dressed in her running gear.

'Where were you?' she said, bouncing impatiently on her toes. 'We were supposed to be meeting downstairs – for our run.'

Our run? I looked at her blankly. It was as if we were on the *Titanic* and she was asking me what dress I was going to wear on the lifeboat.

'I can't run,' I explained. 'I'm having a catastrophe.'

'That's exactly why you *should* run!'

'But if I'm leaving anyway what does it matter?'

'Look. Once you're home, you can do whatever you want. But as long as you're here, we should stick to the programme.'

'Um . . .' I wanted to say no, but there was a steely look in her eyes that I knew all too well.

'I tell you what. Just come out for a walk,' she wheedled. 'Just a ten-minute walk. If, after that, you still don't want to jog – we'll come home.'

'I don't know where all my stuff is,' I said, pathetically.

'Not a problem! Let's make that our next step. All you have to do is put your gear on. Nothing else for now.'

And somehow, I was off the bed and looking for my gear. I rootled in my drawer, and realised my leggings were all in the wash and I'd have to wear the shiny pair that showed my VPL and made my legs look like a pair of black sausages.

'I can't,' I whined. 'These are obscene.'

'Here,' she said, handing me a long T-shirt. 'This covers your booty.'

'Have you ever considered being some kind of military officer, Fletch? You'd be really good at it.'

'No,' she said, stretching her calves. 'I've decided I want to be a doctor.'

'Really?' I said, playing for time. 'That's so interesting! When did you decide that?' With any luck, she'd start chatting and forget what she had come for.

'Well, I—' She paused suddenly. 'I'm on to you. You're not getting me out of a run by chatting. Not this time.'

So we ran. It was a beautiful May morning and it was hard not to feel spirits lift as we jogged – down to Odéon, with its dozens of cinemas and outdoor cafés, down the rue de Seine and past the rue de Buci where the market was in full swing, selling everything from giant peonies to oysters on ice. We passed a string of exquisite art galleries, before we reached the golden dome of the Académie Française, and the Seine.

Once again, Paris struck me in all its ridiculous, impossible beauty. Especially today, in the blinding sunshine that sparkled on the river. All of the chestnut trees were in full bloom. The whole city was blossoming into summer. My heart ached at the thought of leaving all this behind.

'Good going!' Fletcher said. 'Now let's follow the river!'

As we ran along the quays, my stride loosened. I began to dig my heels in further, pump my arms more, work my legs. The famous endorphins were kicking in, almost as if they were massaging my broken heart. With every step, I felt better. More alive, more myself. It was the first time since the Ball that I'd actually been able to breathe properly.

'Hey!' said Fletcher breathlessly, beside me. 'Nice pace!'

I slowed down reluctantly as we went down the steps onto the banks of the Seine. The tourists were going by on their tour boats with the loudspeaker commentary. They were just visiting, but I lived here. For now, anyway.

'Do you want to go home now?' Fletcher asked. I looked at her startled, but then she continued, 'Or can you make it to the next bridge?'

'Oh. Sure. I thought you meant home-home.'

'No . . . I know you've made up your mind on that,' she said.

'I'm really sorry,' I said, uncomfortably. 'I know it leaves you in a bad position.'

'No! That's the last thing you should be worrying about. I'll be totally fine.'

Poor Fletcher! If I was in her position – one of my few good friends at Jean Monnet about to leave – I'd have locked her in her room long before now.

'I'm serious,' she said, looking sideways at me. 'I've moved schools so often. I've been here before. And I always just say to myself: I may not have friends at the moment – but I will have them again in the future.'

We ran on in silence for a minute. I knew Fletcher meant all that in a positive, optimistic way – but it seemed like the saddest thing I'd ever heard.

I didn't know what to say, so I focused on soaking up the sights. The bridges ahead, the river, the winding, never-ending silhouette of the Louvre . . . Soon they'd just be a memory to me, an Instagram feed or a postcard.

'What will you do about the race?' I asked uncertainly.

'Just do it alone. This way you won't hold me back,' she teased.

'Who's holding who back now?' I said, and sprinted ahead. Fletcher laughed, and sprinted with me. Now we were both racing towards the Pont des Invalides, hearts pumping, feet slamming the ground. I felt like I couldn't go on another step, but I did: another and another and another, until I reached it just a few strides ahead of her.

'Nice!' said Fletcher, high-fiving me. 'I totally didn't let you win, by the way. You're faster than me now!'

I was gasping too much to reply. Maybe I'd overdone it. Maybe we needed an ambulance?

'So, we just did,' she looked at her Garmin watch, 'Lola! Did you see what we did? Eight miles! That's two miles further than we need to run at the race!'

'Wow,' I panted. 'Really?' This was actually quite thrilling. We started walking up the steps towards the bridge. I felt terrible; I felt fantastic.

'It's great when it stops, isn't it?' Fletcher grinned.

I nodded, still incapable of speech.

'You know what else?' she said slyly. 'I bet, if you did stay and do the race ... We could make it a half marathon.'

'A half marathon? That's thirteen miles!'

'Sure,' she said. 'But you just did eight with very little effort. We've got two more weeks, so you could get up to ten. And on the day of the race – I *know* you could do more. We could still change our registration. Come on! Wouldn't that be a trip?'

Laughing, I said, 'You're crazy!' But I thought how much I was going to miss her. And Paris. And running.

The irony wasn't lost on me. I came to Paris because I was running away. Now I was running away *from* Paris. Would I be on the run for the rest of my life? Where would it end? No matter where I went or what I was called, I could never get away from myself.

Now that we'd stopped running, I was exhausted. My legs were suddenly aching, my face was red ... but I felt great. And I knew what I had to do.

'I'm going to stay,' I told her.

Fletcher stopped short, almost knocking over man walking a poodle.

'Are you sure?' she said.

'I've got to stop running eventually,' I said. 'If you catch my drift.'

Her eyes narrowed suspiciously. 'You're not just staying to be nice to me, are you? That would be too nice. And you're always lecturing me about being too nice . . .'

'No!' I said. 'And you know what else?'

'What?'

I glanced back at the route we'd already travelled and then further up the river. If I could suffer through this week, I could suffer through an extra five miles.

'We're doing the half marathon.'

Fletcher's cheers and shrieks attracted the stares of a boatful of tourists, while I hoped I hadn't said goodbye to what remained of my sanity.

Chapter fifty-eight

The promise of the race was one of a few bright spots in a truly horrible week. Not only did I have exams looming; my life felt as if it was hanging by a very, very thin thread.

Kiyoshi and I had an awkward conversation or two. He was confused, more than angry. He was also wrapped up with Marco Agnelli. I would see them drifting around the courtyard together, sharing an earbud each and listening to music on one of their phones. I would have been really happy for him if I hadn't been so lonely.

'It was supposed to be ironic,' I told him, for the millionth time.

'I know,' he said, uncertainly. 'I guess, if you'd said that at the start, we would have got it maybe. It's just the fact that you made up a new name for yourself. And lied to us all. People feel a bit freaked out.'

I hung my head. 'I understand.'

And at least Kiyoshi would speak to me. Vee ignored me totally. She literally looked right through me, walked past me, even pushed past me once – her icy face in contrast with the very huge, OTT hat that she was wearing. I couldn't help but think, though, that it could have been worse. If Vee had been around in the days when they threw things at people in stocks, I betted she would have been first in line with her eggs.

I made a discovery, though. The worst thing – the thing I'd been dreading – had happened, and I survived. I had been unmasked in front of the whole school; now I had nothing more to fear.

My other discovery was: you only really needed one friend. As long as you had one person who was totally on your side – like I had Fletcher – you would basically be fine. I knew that no matter what happened, she and I would be friends for a long time. Which made me feel happy, but also deeply sad, because that was what I had once thought about Tariq.

Chapter fifty-nine

My Skype calls home had become a nightly ritual by now. They helped a bit – except that Mum was actually driving me crazy. She was obsessed with finding silver linings in the black storm cloud of my life. So far she had come up with the following:

1. At least it was out in the open now.
2. At least I still had one friend.
3. At least I'd learned some French.

Honestly. What was next? 'At least you've had some pretty tasty Nutella crepes.' 'At least you haven't been arrested.'

'Well,' Mum was saying. 'One good thing is the timing. It's nearly the end of term – it'll probably all be forgotten over the summer.'

'Mum,' I said through gritted teeth. 'Can you please *stop* pointing out all the good things in this situation? Because from where I'm sitting, there aren't any.'

'There are always good things,' Mum said, upset. 'In any situation.'

'No! Actually, sometimes there aren't!' I said. 'Or if there are, let me decide that! You're not in my situation! Stop telling me how great it is and just listen to me for once when I tell you that it's not! STOP TELLING ME HOW I FEEL!'

Mum said nothing. The screen paused on her startled face.

'Mum?' I said.

The screen stayed frozen. Now I was alarmed. Had I actually broken Skype with my rage?

Then it flickered back. She was still there, albeit a bit shell-shocked.

'Did you get all of that?' I said, feeling stupid.

'Yes, love, I did.' She looked remorseful. 'I really did. And I'm so sorry. I didn't realise quite how I was coming across. I was just trying to help.'

'Yes, but the more you tell me that everything's great, the worse it makes it!' I could feel myself getting wound up again. 'Why can't you just agree with me that things are bad sometimes? Then I would feel better!'

'Because I can't stand it. I can't stand things to go wrong for you.'

'Well, you're going to have to,' I said. 'Because they will. That's just life.'

Mum laughed. 'You sound like your Gran. You know, she always used to wind me up because she was such a negative person. Everything was terrible, everything was doom and gloom. That's probably why I wanted to work in PR – just to hear some good news for a change.'

247

'She sounds like a smart woman,' I said snippily. 'I'm sorry I never knew her. Oh, God, Mum, don't cry.'

'I'm fine! It's fine,' Mum said, wiping her eyes. 'It's just been a long week. Look, I am sorry if you feel I'm not listening. I probably do overdo it sometimes, with the positivity. I'll try and listen to you more.'

'Thanks,' I muttered.

'By the way, I bumped into your friend Ellie the other day. In a shoe shop. She was with her mum.'

'Oh?' I said nervously.

'She was asking after you,' Mum said, to my surprise. 'She said she'd love to hear from you.'

'Are you sure?' I said, dubious. 'Mum, this isn't you being positive again, is it?'

'No, Delilah, it isn't. She said to tell you hello and that you should get in touch. Lenny – shush. Sorry, love. I think he wants to talk to you. Yes, you do! Well why were you hanging around then? Here she is.'

Lenny didn't appear for ages, and then his face loomed at one corner. The image lurched around then, and I could see he was taking me to 'his' room.

'That wall still looks awful,' I told him, as he settled onto his bed.

'Well, if you'd stayed, I wouldn't have painted it, would I?'

'*Painted* is a strong word,' I said. 'It looks more like you dipped your tail in paint.'

Lenny immediately sat up, turned round, and shoved his rear end towards the camera.

'Noo!' I yelled. 'Stop! Pervert.' Without me to keep an eye on him, his behaviour was just out of control.

He turned round, grinning, and sat down. 'Don't worry, Delinquent. I wasn't going to moon you.'

I sighed. 'Look, Len. I am sorry about everything that's happened. Honestly. I never really thought that it's been horrible for you too.'

He lifted his shoulders to his ears.

'S'OK,' he said, after a pause. His mouth twitched at the corner. 'I *did* get a Segway out of it.'

'Yeah. I want a go on that, when I come home.'

'When are you coming home?'

'When terms ends. Duh.'

'But are you going back there again next year?'

'I don't know,' I admitted. That was the big unknown. I changed my mind about it every day, but right now I was leaning towards *no freaking way*.

'If you do,' Lenny said, 'I reckon I might get an iPad.'

Chapter sixty

After I had hung up, I couldn't stop thinking about what Mum had said about seeing Ellie. And about Ellie saying that she'd love to hear from me.

It probably wasn't true at all. It was just Mum doing her usual over-optimistic thing. She had probably said, 'You two should get in touch' and Ellie had just agreed to be polite, or something. If only Lenny had been there – he could tell me.

I tried to think of the last contact I had with Ellie – was it a text, Snapchat or what? If only I still had my old phone I could have pinged her a quick message. I did remember her mobile number though.

I shivered. Could I actually do that? Just phone her? It seemed so weird.

But what did I have to lose? The worst she could do was hang up on me. Or we would have a horribly awkward conversation and that would be that.

I sat on the edge of my bed and found myself dialling her number . . . This is a crazy idea, I thought, and I half-hoped that she wouldn't answer.

'Hello?'

'Ellie,' I had to clear my throat. 'It's me. It's . . . Delilah.'

There was a pause that felt as if it lasted forever. Then she said, 'Delilah! Where *are* you? Are you OK?

Her voice sounded so familiar, as if we'd chatted the night before. I smiled. 'I'm in Paris.'

'In *Paris*? How did you end up there?'

'Well, it's kind of a long story. Have you got time?'

And before long we were chatting away – as if nothing had changed, even though everything had. She caught me up on all the gossip at home, and I tried to describe my life in Paris to her. I didn't mention Tariq, though. The old me would have blurted it out right away, but I knew it wasn't the right time.

'A race?' she said, when I mentioned my training. 'You're running? God, Delilah – you *have* changed.'

'Is that a good thing?' I asked uncomfortably. 'I mean – I did wonder what happened with us. Why we stopped speaking.'

'We didn't stop speaking. You stopped replying to our messages.'

'No, I didn't!'

'Well, that's what it felt like. Though – maybe we could have tried harder. But the thing is, Del, you were just so—'

Now we were getting somewhere. 'So . . . what?'

'You were a bit full of yourself,' Ellie said. 'It felt like you were looking down on us because you were a prefect, and you were tweeting about politics and we were just wasting our lives doing stupid duck-face selfies.'

'I never said that!' But I realised, with a guilty feeling, that I had been *thinking* that. I didn't know it had come across so clearly.

'I'm so sorry ,' I said.

'I know,' she said immediately. 'I'm sorry too. We didn't think enough about what it was like for you. Honestly, we just didn't know how to handle it all. But I think it will be different, when we see you.'

'When you see me?'

'Well, yeah. We'll be here for at least a few weeks after A-Levels . . . You'll be coming back for the holidays, won't you?' She seemed to hesitate. 'Or maybe I could visit you in Paris?'

'That would be really cool,' I said, my voice shaking with happiness.

We talked for a while longer before we put down the phone. After all the months of worry and sadness, I couldn't believe how easy that had been. It was as if we'd never been apart. True friends. As I tidied away my trainers and took out my laptop, I smiled at Ellie's amazement at my running.

Then I had another thought. If things had resolved so easily with Ellie – maybe there was also some hope for me and Tariq?

Chapter sixty-one

On Friday evening, I took my courage in both hands. I could see, from the light on the other side of the courtyard, that Tariq was in his room. So I walked round to the boys' corridor and knocked on his door.

I had never really spent much time in his room, but I knew what it looked like – very tidy, with tons of books and extra room for his extensive wardrobe. No piles of socks or half-eaten pizzas. A few film posters on the wall, actually framed and hung with picture hooks, instead of Blu-Tak, completed the grown-up effect. The only thing that looked different was his expression. He looked as uncomfortable as I felt.

'Hi,' he said.

'Tariq,' I said miserably. 'I am really sorry that I lied to everyone. But I truly didn't mean – what I said. I was hoping . . .' I swallowed. 'I was hoping we could be friends again.'

'It's not that I don't believe you,' he said.

My heart thumped. He believed me!

'But the thing is, I have to be really careful about things like this.'

'What?'

'I mean with the election coming,' he said.

I stared at him. I could have understood him feeling angry about what I said, feeling betrayed, or taking it personally. But to hang me out to dry because of the election . . . I just couldn't believe it.

'It's not that we can't hang out ever again, or anything,' he was saying. 'I just need to be careful – for the next week or so. I'm sure you understand . . .'

'I understand,' I said. I turned round and walked straight back to my room. Amazingly, I didn't cry. I was too angry and bewildered. How could I have been so wrong about him – about everything? At least that way, *his* real self had been exposed too.

Chapter sixty-two

It turned out that I had finally discovered the secret to avoiding exam stress.

Just make sure you get publicly disgraced, lose all your friends and the potential love of your life. You'll be so busy contemplating the ruins of your life, everything else will seem fine.

I had never paid so little attention to exams. I did some study when I had the brain space, but that was it. To say I was phoning it in would be generous. I was Whatsapping it in with emojis; I was typing a tweet with one finger. I was far more concerned with Race Day, which was on the Saturday before the last week of term. It also happened to be the day of the student election, which was a happy coincidence. It meant I could escape the whole circus and not have to watch Tariq avoid me either.

Fletcher and I weren't meeting until seven, but I had slept really badly, so at six a.m., I decided to stop staring at the ceiling and get out of bed. My kit was all laid out for me: anti-blister socks, my favourite sports bra and leggings, plus the top we'd been sent in the post. Fletcher had insisted on getting transfer letters to iron our names on – so that people in the crowd could yell our names. Mine said Lola on it, of course.

'I don't know if I can wear this,' I'd said to Fletcher, when she produced it.

She shrugged. 'Well, it's too late now. I don't have enough letters to do Delilah.'

I couldn't really argue with that.

Anyway, it seemed sort of appropriate. It wasn't Delilah who put in all those training miles and got up every morning to run before school. It was Lola. Just like it was Lola who'd coped with a new school, and learned her way around the metro, and fallen for Paris and Tariq. And even learned to like sushi. Maybe I *was* Lola now. I certainly wasn't completely Delilah any more.

With my kit on, I took a minute to look at myself and marvel at what had happened. A few months ago, I couldn't run more than a mile, and now ... I had a favourite sports bra. And a runner's form. I turned sideways to the mirror, realising that I did look different now. I hadn't been fat before, but I didn't have much tone or muscle. Now I was leaner, fitter. Stronger. It was a good feeling.

We met in reception at seven, and slipped out of school just as people were gathering for breakfast.

'Don't forget to cast your ballots today!' an officious-looking IB Two was saying, waving envelopes around.

I hesitated, torn. Fletcher was already taking her form and envelope. I could abstain, obviously. Or if I wanted to be really evil, I could vote for Hunter.

But I didn't want to do either of those things. I was going to try and be grown-up about all this, even though my world was falling apart. I hated Tariq now, but I agreed with his policies. I ticked the box beside his name, and stuffed the envelope back into the ballot box, under the beady eye of the IB Two girl. You would have thought she was monitoring us on behalf of the UN or something.

'Did you vote for Tariq?' Fletcher asked me, as we walked up rue Vaugirard to the metro.

I nodded. 'Did you?'

'Of course. I hope he gets in. I know he's a dead cert, but on the other hand, if everyone thinks that, then the turnout might be low, and he might not get elected.'

'Mm.' That was the exact same thing Tariq told me. I had thought he was confiding in me, but it was part of his election tactics. I knew he was a politician, but still; it was depressing. Oh, well. It was another bitter lesson to learn. I just hoped there would come a day – in the not so far future – when I didn't have to *keep* learning lessons.

'So you probably haven't had breakfast either,' Fletcher said. 'Look what I brought!'

She produced a paper bag with two croissants, and I snarfed one down. It was against all the proper race-nutrition rules but, as Fletcher said, we were in France after all.

'Also, this isn't a marathon,' she reminded me, as we got on the metro. 'A half is long, but it's nothing you can't handle.'

I wasn't so sure. It was still thirteen point something miles; four miles further than I'd ever run in my life. I had wanted to go those extra miles during training but

Fletcher was adamant that there wasn't time and we should 'taper off' instead – reduce our training to rest up in advance of the race.

'Look!' she said, nudging me.

Expecting a celebrity spot or at least a gorgeous guy, I glanced up. A bunch of other people were getting on the metro wearing their tell-tale blue T-shirts. Grinning at Fletcher, I began to feel the excitement of being part of something bigger than our little runs together, bigger than school even.

The race was in the Bois de Boulogne, a park on the western outskirts of Paris, full of woods and boating lakes. The crowd there was of all shapes, sizes and ability, wearing everything from serious runner's gear to novelty costumes. Looking at a grey-haired woman taping up her ankle, I thought: if she can do this, I can. Mind you, a line of ambulances and a few big First Aid tents presented an alternative scenario.

It was an international race, with runners from the UK and America – luckily for us, because it meant that there were mile markers as well the main signage in kilometres. We had done all our training in miles, and if I'd had to pace myself *and* do metric conversions in my head, I would have imploded.

'Ugh,' said Fletcher, bouncing on one leg. 'I need to pee – *again* – but check out that line.' She nodded to where twenty female runners stood patiently outside three portaloos.

'Use the men's,' I suggested. I didn't think for a second that she would, but she did; nipping to the queue and back out, within five minutes. Laughing, we ran off to find our places. You had to give a rough prediction of your speed so that they could stagger the starts, so we were in the section that was between two hours and two hours fifteen. Personally, I thought that Fletcher had been pretty optimistic about our chances.

Now we were in our places. Everyone was laughing, chatting, exchanging smiles, full of nervous good-will. My stomach started to clench again with fear. What if I broke an ankle? What if my legs gave out at mile six?

'Then you get first aid, and we meet at the finish,' said Fletcher, when I voiced my fears to her. 'But you won't. You'll be awesome.'

Easily said. But it was too late now. I hadn't heard a starting gun, but like a flock of birds, the crowd began to move together, and we were off. My legs and arms found their familiar rhythm. After a painful five or ten minutes, my limbs felt loose and easy. Suddenly I thought: I can do this.

'Easy, tiger,' said Fletcher. 'Miles one to six are our warm-up, remember?'

She was right. I could already feel the temptation to sprint ahead, to gobble up the miles while I could. But it was crucial that we pace ourselves. I tried to focus on all the sights around me; the sunlight coming through the trees, the lake in the distance with the boats, the hundreds of runners moving alongside me in harmony. I found myself thinking about all kinds of things; my friends at home; Tariq and how it all went wrong.

But then my mind switched off and I started to get into that magic flow state where my mind was easy and calm, and I felt as if I was floating along, independent of the effort my legs and arms were making. Way before I was expecting her to, Fletcher called out, 'Mile six!'

'Already?' I said exuberantly. 'That was nothing!' And it had felt like nothing. Except that, of course, we had to do that all over again – and then some.

Mile seven. I was starting to feel conscious of lots of different unpleasant things: a nagging pain in my knee; a sore foot, probably with a blister. My sports bra was starting to chafe. We were coming up to mile eight and I shivered. Beyond this was unknown territory.

'Sorry, Fletch. My stupid sock . . . I'll catch you up.'

She nodded, too out of breath to talk. I stooped down to apply my blister bandage, blessing Fletcher for making me take it. After taping my foot, I started again.

But the break had been fatal. The flow was gone, and I felt like the Tin Man. My knees were both complaining; my arms were made of cotton wool. My bra was still chafing, really sharply now, but there was nothing I could do about it. I gritted my teeth and kept plugging on, focusing on Fletcher's ponytail in the distance. The patch of sweat on her back had tripled in size.

'Ugh – finally,' I panted, when I caught her up at long last. 'Sorry.'

'No probs,' she said, breathlessly. 'How's your foot?'

'Bit sore.'

We slogged on. My effortless floating feeling of earlier had totally gone. I was struggling to put one foot in front of another. My thoughts contracted to a tiny world of pain and fatigue. Sore foot. Sore bra. Tired feet. Tired everything. I saw someone sitting down to tie his shoe and fantasised about the act of sitting. Delicious sitting! Why had I never appreciated it before?

Mile eight. Time to stop. I knew now that this half marathon had been a crazy idea. I should never, ever have agreed to it. I hated myself for signing up, and I even began to hate Fletcher for putting me though it.

'How you doing?' said Fletcher. She was still plugging along effortlessly, making me feel even worse.

'Not . . . great,' I said. 'I'm actually thinking I can't go on much further.'

'Yes. You can. You could go on for another six miles, if you had to. Imagine if there was a gun to your head.'

'Thanks.'

'I'm serious,' she panted. 'You're so much . . . stronger . . . than you think you are.'

We limped on for another age, while Fletcher panted out more inspirational talk. I wasn't listening any more. I would have loved a drink of water but the effort of trying to find one was beyond me. Plus, my knees really hurt.

'One knee or both?' Fletcher said sharply, when I told her. When I said both, she said that was fine. The twisted logic of runners.

'One knee would be an injury, but two sounds more like pain. Don't think of it as pain, though,' Fletcher said. 'Just think of it as . . . A sensation.'

Holy moley. She was like Superwoman. It did help, though. I started to tune out of the pain. It would stop eventually. It was just a sensation.

'What mile . . . are we on now?' I asked.

'Nearly mile ten,' panted Fletcher. 'That's our walking mile.' She had promised earlier that we would walk for the whole of mile ten.

We were passing a small group huddled around a runner, who was being loaded onto a stretcher. It was a sobering reminder; this was serious stuff. We were putting big demands on ourselves – and I wasn't sure I was up to it.

When our walking mile came, mile ten, came, I almost cried with relief. I was aching all over, as if I'd been beaten up. But all too soon, mile eleven came and we had to start running again.

'Come on. We've done most of it,' Fletcher said. 'We're so nearly there. Only three more miles!'

I nodded and put my head down and powered on, even more determined.

But my brief burst of will soon wore out. The thought of mile twelve and thirteen, taunting us in the distance, just felt too much. This isn't fun, I thought. This is torture. Why did I ever, ever, sign up for this? Everything was awful. I hated everything and everyone. Even the cheering crowds calling us on made me upset, because nobody was cheering for us.

'Lola!' Fletcher said. She patted my arm without breaking her stride. 'Come on. You're hitting the wall – that's all. But I *know* you can do it. I *know* you can.'

I shook my head. My pace had slowed to a limp. I kept slowing to a walk, then a painful half-jog. All I wanted was to sit down. And not get up again, ever.

'If you can finish this race, you can do anything in life. I'm serious. *Anything*.'

Sure. *If* I could do this – then yes, that would be great. But what if I couldn't?

A man in the crowd leaned forward. '*Allez . . . Fletchair!*' he said, giving us a double thumbs-up. '*Allez, Lola!*'

The effect of hearing our names was electric. We were both too knackered even to wave to him, but we broke into big grins. I dug my heels in. I tried to breathe more deeply, and move my arms more, which Fletcher had advised me to do when my legs wore out. Before long, somehow, I was running again. This must be what they meant by the second wind.

'Mile twelve!' gasped Fletch. 'We'll be at mile thirteen in *ten minutes*, Lola!'

I nodded, too exhausted to say anything. I just had to keep moving. Keep moving. Keep moving. I plastered a smile onto my face, which was another Fletcher tactic, and it helped. I repeated to myself, 'It's not pain . . . it's a sensation. A sensation.' It worked. Either I was hallucinating, or else I could see mile thirteen now.

'So close!' Fletch panted, beside me. 'So close!' I wasn't sure if she was speaking to me or to herself.

My foot was agony now with every step; I was positive my back was bleeding from my bra. But I kept on, pace after pace after pace. I could see the finish line. I could hear the crowd, roaring louder and louder. We could have been running for two hours; it could have been six. I could only think of putting one foot in front of the other.

'We're almost there!' screamed Fletcher, above the noise of the spectators. The finish line was maybe forty paces away. Forty paces more than I had in me, but I ran them anyway. There was a lump in my throat. Twenty. Ten. Five more paces, and I could stop.

'We did it!' Fletcher shrieked. As we crossed the finish line, I started to cry.

'Oh, Lola, come on! We did it!' Fletch said. 'Merci!' she added to a race assistant, who was putting a medal around both our necks. I couldn't open my mouth to thank him. I could barely stay upright.

'Oh my God, look,' I heard Fletcher say.

A familiar face, but smiling – the way I hadn't seen him smile all week.

'Lola!' Tariq said. 'Well done! Hey – don't cry!'

He reached out for me. Sobbing harder now, I folded into his arms.

Chapter sixty-three

We didn't kiss. We couldn't, with Fletcher standing there, not to mention with me in such a revolting state. But he hugged us both, and kissed my cheek. I felt his lips graze the edge of my mouth, and it sent shocks of electricity through me that powered me, briefly, out of my bone-weary state.

'How did you – what are you doing here?' I managed to say. The voting went on all day; surely he should be there?

'Supporting you at the finish line.' He turned to Fletcher, who was grinning broadly at us both. 'Nice job!'

Being Tariq, he had thought to bring two bottles of ice-cold sports drinks, which we gulped down.

'Let's see those medals,' he said.

They were engraved with the date, and the name of the race, and a picture of a little runner. I looked at it in wonder.

'We did it,' I said to Fletcher. She grinned at me, and we both wrapped each other in a huge hug.

'You are a rock star,' she said.

'You too,' I muttered in her ear. She hugged me back, harder, and when she drew back we were both tearful.

'Come on,' Fletcher said, wiping her eyes. 'Let's check out all the free stuff!'

The finish had a carnival atmosphere. Stalls were giving away healthy freebies – nutrition balls, bars and shakes – but since this was Paris, there were also crepes, ice creams and even a little cheese stall. We all wanted ice creams, but the queues were daunting.

'Let me get these,' Tariq said. 'You two go and sit down.'

'Can I have a pistachio one?' I said. 'No, make it mint and pistachio.'

'Let me give you some money,' Fetcher said.

'Fletcher,' he said warningly, and we all laughed.

We went and collapsed under a tree. I was still feeling exhausted, but also exhilarated. The pleasure of not having to run any more felt like a drug.

'Well. You two seemed pleased to see each other.'

'Yes.' I bit my lip to stop myself smiling.

'Is there something you want to tell me, Lola?'

I shook my head, too tired to explain. But my stupid grin probably said it all.

'Should I leave you to it?' she said, suddenly sounding uncertain.

'No!' I was dying to talk to Tariq alone, but there was no way I was abandoning Fletcher now.

Tariq was coming back now with our ice-creams. Seeing him approach us, in his white T-shirt and jeans, took my breath away all over again. Not just because he looked so beautiful – but because he was here, for me.

'Let me take a picture of you two Olympians,' Tariq said, once the ice-creams had reduced me and Fletcher to speechlessness.

He snapped us both with his phone. Then he leaned in beside us, for a selfie.

'I might post this on the school Facebook page. If that's OK with you two?'

I stared at him. If he posted a picture with me . . .

'Tariq,' I said. 'What about the election? People won't have finished voting yet.'

'I don't care about the election,' he said. And posted it.

Chapter sixty-four

We spent another half-hour at the finish, before we dragged ourselves home on the metro.

'What now?' Tariq said, when we were back at Jean Monnet.

'A shower,' I said. 'I can't believe they let me on the metro like this.'

'Me too,' said Fletcher. 'And then I have some study to do. A lot of study.' She turned to me, raising her eyebrows. 'But you should probably keep walking around, Lola. You don't want to get stiff.'

I turned to go too, but Tariq pulled me back by the hand.

'I'll wait for you down here,' he said.

I was torn between taking ages to get cute, and impatience to be with him. Impatience won, and soon I was back downstairs, with no make-up except mascara, and damp hair in a bun. He was still waiting for me in reception.

We started walking towards the Jardin du Luxembourg. As we crossed the rue Vaugirard he took my hand. Once we were inside the park – where I'd jogged with Fletch all those weeks ago – he turned to me and kissed me again, properly. As we strolled through the park, under the chestnut trees with their white candles, I had to pinch myself.

'Come on – let's go to the Medici fountain,' he said.

I'd never been here before. It was a lovely, shady spot. A long, mossy basin overflowed with water, watched over by a huge statue of an angry figure bearing down on an unfortunate couple.

'Who are these guys?' I asked. 'It looks like M. Mougel walking in on a couple making out.'

'I don't know. Doesn't matter. Come here.' He pulled me close. If I thought our first kiss was the one to end all kisses, I was wrong.

'I'm sorry, Lola,' he said eventually. For a horrible second I thought he meant he wanted to stop, but then I realised what he meant.

'Why did you react like that?' I asked.

'I'll be honest. I was worried about what people would think. But I was also offended. I really try not to let stuff like that get to me. I try not to play the race card. But I *was* angry.'

'I know.'

'Do you?' he said drily. 'It's just that feeling that someone sees you for you . . . and then you realise, oh. That's how they see me. As one of a group or a category. One of *them*.'

I nodded sadly.

'But then I read up on the whole thing . . . and I realised you were just trying to be witty. You dork.'

'Thanks,' I said. I was trying to be sarcastic, but there was a lump in my throat.

'Lola, please don't cry!' He hugged me, and then we started kissing again. No matter how often we did this . . . I would never, ever get tired of it.

'Tariq,' I said eventually. 'Can I ask you something?'

'Yes. As long as it's not going to be about some guy you have a crush on, who keeps sending you messages.'

'What? Oh.' Of course; my question on behalf of Kiyoshi. 'I *told* you that was for a friend . . .'

'Asking for a friend. Sure. Well, I wasn't sure at the time. Which was probably why I didn't ask you to the ball. That, and feeling bad for Fletcher.' He sighed. 'I am a bit of a coward. I don't like entering competitions unless I'm sure I can win. Not that you're a competition, but you know what I mean.'

I shook my head, thinking how illogical people were.

'What were you going to ask me?'

I said shyly, 'Just . . . are you sure you're not on the rebound from Priscilla?'

'From Priscilla? No.' I felt a bit better as I saw how confidently he shook his head. 'Look, Priscilla was great, and I'm not going to start criticising her now that we've broken up.'

I nodded, thinking that a *little* bit of criticism wouldn't hurt right now.

'But you said you only broke up with her because of the distance . . .'

'That wasn't completely true,' he admitted. 'The thing is, we'd been together for so long – we really were more like brother and sister towards the end. Or good friends, anyway. Maybe we're too similar.' He smiled, brushing the hair away from my face. 'Whereas you . . . I don't know anyone else who would get drunk by themselves at lunchtime. Or make up their own language. Or hang out with me on the rooftop on a week night. Or invent a whole new identity for themselves and go on the run . . .'

'Oh, no,' I said, dismayed. 'Is that how you see me? A Manic Dream Pixie Girl?'

'A what? No! Look, compared to me, you're on the – dreamier spectrum. Compared to someone like Vee, you're straight-edge. It's all relative. You're just yourself. And I like that.' He leaned in again, and kissed me.

After a while, he said, 'Deja ta windeth . . .'

I stared in astonishment. He remembered Delilish!

He paused, and then clicked his fingers. 'That's "Do you want to go", isn't it? I don't know "out with me tonight".

'Tariq, everybody in this school is going to hate you for dating me,' I said, once we'd stopped kissing again.

'No, they won't. And if they do, I don't care.'

I looked at him sceptically. Surely everyone cared what people thought – especially him?

'I'm serious. I've realised that it's no way to live – worrying about your image all the time. If they don't like it, they can do one. As you English say.'

He was grinning at me. God, how I had missed that grin.

'You know what I want to suggest, don't you?'

'What?' I said warily.

'Community meeting.'

'What? No! Public humiliation, you mean.'

'No! A chance to put across your side of the story.' He took my hand. 'I'd be there. And Fletcher.'

'And Vee, and Priya, and everyone else who hates me . . .' I felt suddenly doubtful. Was this his way of making me acceptable again? Would he still want to be with me, if I didn't go through the ritual humiliation?

'I don't think I can.'

'Fine. You don't have to. I just—' Was that a blush on the unflappable Tariq's face? 'I just want you to be happy.'

I realised he meant it. Which meant I would think about it.

But meanwhile, we had a serious amount of kissing to catch up on.

Chapter sixty-five

I thought about it all night.

On a logical level, I supposed it was probably the right thing to do. It would allow me to put across my side of the story. And it was true that when I had told the full story – to Fletcher, or to Tariq, over dinner last night – they understood.

But that was when I was talking to friends. I wasn't sure how it would work in a big, formal setting like the school hall. What if I messed it up, or made myself sound worse than ever?

And it wasn't just that. Even if everyone got it and was supportive, that wouldn't be my happy ever after. I would still always have to explain this thing. It would always come up when I was googled. It would follow me around for the rest of my life.

Then I remembered something Tariq had said last night. He said, 'If you don't tell your own story, other people will tell it for you.' I knew what he meant. But I was not at all sure that I could actually do it.

Chapter sixty-six

The Student Council elections results were announced the next day, Sunday. I wanted to lie low, but Tariq insisted on sitting with me and Fletcher at lunch and then keeping me superglued to him, practically, during the 'count' – the big election party that took place out in the courtyard. But there was one person I did want to talk to.

I waited until Vee was on her own, and then walked right up to her.

'Before you say anything – just listen. I'm sorry that I lied to you. You were my friend and you deserved better.'

Vee nodded. She didn't say anything, so I continued, 'How did you find out?'

She just shook her head. 'Come on,' she said. 'It's all over the internet. Google "racist teenager" and you're on the first page. Second page, maybe.'

'Right.' Of course. That was exactly the kind of thing Vee would google.

'Look. I should apologise too.'

'Really?' This was a surprise.

Looking furiously into the distance, Vee said, 'I was jealous, I suppose. You suddenly had all these new friends, and you were obsessed with your running . . . We used to hang out so much but then you disappeared.'

'I didn't disappear! I just made other friends.' What was I supposed to do? Not speak to anyone but her, and live in her pocket all the time? It reminded me of being fourteen, and it made me tired.

I wanted to say all this to her, but there was no point. I hadn't realised, up until now, how deeply insecure she was.

'I'm sorry you felt that way,' I said. And I was. But all the same, I was relieved to see her go and join Kiyoshi and Priya.

'Everything OK?' Tariq said, coming up to me.

'It's complicated.'

Tariq looked at me sympathetically. Then he said, 'I've spoken to Ms Curtis. They can make a slot for you at the next community meeting. But no pressure.'

My heart sank again. Looking around at everyone else laughing and chatting, being *normal*, I couldn't imagine any of them wanting to hear my story.

But then I remembered little Felipe, on my first week here – going up to the podium with his too-high trousers, knees shaking together. If he could do it, I could do it.

'Fine,' I said. 'Count me in.'

Chapter sixty-seven

It was Monday morning. The final week of school; there were no more classes and a lot of sunbathing, packing and discussing of holiday plans. But there was still quite a crowd gathered in the assembly hall as I took my place at the podium. I saw Vee and Kiyoshi with Marco Agnelli. I couldn't see Tariq, but that was because he was on the platform beside me, as the Student President elect.

It was, quite frankly, the stuff of nightmares.

'Hi. You all know me as Lola, but that's not my real name. My name is Delilah Hoover . . .'

I couldn't even focus on the words I was saying. I kept on having lucid-dream moments where I realised that yes, I really was speaking in front of the entire school. And yes, there were hundreds of pairs of eyes all fixed on me.

'It started when I was on Twitter. I saw something horrible that someone had written, about these students . . .'

More stares. I caught Vee's eye for a split second before she stared away.

'I really wanted to defend them all, but I also wanted to say something witty.'

I swallowed. This was the first time I'd admitted that out loud.

'So I wrote . . . the tweet that you've all seen.' I had to stop then, to catch my breath. 'I was trying to be witty, and ironic. I was going to hashtag it "stuff stupid white people say" but I didn't. I thought it would be cooler not to.'

As I described what had happened in the days and weeks after Twittergate, the audience became very still. I could see that none of them had imagined it was that bad.

'So, after talking to my parents, I decided I couldn't go back to school . . .' I started to speed up more nervously. But a little smile from Kiyoshi in the audience made me feel calmer.

'. . . So I ended up here.' I found myself running out of words, and looked over to Ms Curtis for guidance. She nodded, which I decided was my cue to stop. Everyone was still gazing at me as I walked away from the podium. There was some polite applause, which seemed to be led by the teachers, but it didn't sound very heartfelt.

It hadn't worked. They didn't believe me. Without looking back, I hurried out of the room through the side door, as quickly as I could.

What a fool I was. I had thought that I'd get up there, give a big speech and feel like a weight had been lifted off me . . . but it had made no difference. Except maybe to make things worse.

'Lola!' It was Fletcher. She came crashing through the door of the ladies' to find me bent over the sink. 'What's wrong? Everyone's clapping! You were great!'

'They're still clapping?'

'Yes! Didn't you hear them? It took a while to start but that's because we didn't know if you were finished or not. But everyone thinks you did awesome!'

I came out with her into the corridor. A young girl with a long ponytail, who I vaguely recognised, was waiting there.

'I just have to tell you . . . The same thing happened to me,' she said. 'I mean not exactly the same thing, but I made a stupid joke about a plane accident, and I got trolled. It was so horrible. I know exactly how you feel.'

Another girl, equally young, materialised beside her. 'My little sister was in a changing room and someone took a picture of her and put it on Snapchat. She was twelve. I know how you feel.'

'No, but – she didn't do anything wrong. I did.'

'I don't think you did,' said Fletcher.

'It wasn't that bad. It was just, like, not great judgement,' said Ponytail Girl, who had to be all of fourteen.

'Come on,' said the other girl, in a motherly way.

Back in the hall, Ms Curtis was standing at the podium, saying something. Seeing me, she broke off. 'Ah – there she is. People; let's show our support for Delilah – or Lola.'

And they all started clapping. And smiling. Kiyoshi gave me a thumbs-up and even Vee gave me a little smile and a nod. Overwhelmed, I nodded and smiled at everyone, before slinking back to my seat.

'That wasn't so bad, was it?' Fletcher said, radiant beside me.

'Um,' I said. 'No, I suppose not.' I felt giddy with relief and exhaustion – the way I felt when we finished the race.

I knew this wasn't the only time I would have to explain myself. I'd have to do it many, many times over in the future. But now that I knew how to do it, I hoped the next time would be easier – and the time after that.

'Well done,' said Tariq, beside me. 'That was really great.'

I wanted to throw myself into his arms, but I was too self-conscious of doing it in front of the whole school. He wasn't, though. Before I knew it, I was wrapped in his arms. I noticed a few people looking at us, but he was paying them zero attention, so I did the same.

'I think that deserves a crepe. Would you agree?' he asked me.

I nodded gratefully.

Neither of us had class. School was basically over, and Paris was all ours. Until I had to go home – but I was hoping to spin out my time here as long as I could. Tariq was staying here over the summer, and I still hadn't been up the Eiffel Tower.

'So – what should I call you now?' he said, taking my hand.

'How do you mean?' I said, smiling.

'Well – I know you as Lola. But now I know you're . . . really Delilah? Technically Delilah? Which do you prefer?'

I let out a sigh. The truth was I didn't exactly feel like Delilah any more. I wasn't the same person who arrived in Paris with newly dyed hair and a fake name.

'I'm starting to prefer Lola,' I admitted. 'But I know that's not really, officially me.'

'OK,' he said.

'So . . . maybe I'll stay Delilah Hoover officially – but have Lola as a nickname. Do you think that would work?'

Tariq leaned in and kissed me. 'Of course.'

I smiled. I was beginning to feel, for the first time in a long time, that things might – just might – be OK. More than OK. Online, and offline.

Acknowledgments

Nobody can do anything entirely on their own, let alone publish a book. A big thank-you to the brilliant team at Hachette especially Felicity Johnston, Jennie Skinner, Helen Thomas, Julia Sanderson, Stephanie Stahl and Stephanie Allen. Thank you to the perennially wonderful Rowan Lawton, Liane-Louise Smith and Isha Karki at Furniss Lawton: I can't believe this is our fifth book together! Thanks to Neil Allen, Jennifer Thompson, Mayuri Perera and the students and staff of the International School of Brussels, who welcomed me to their beautiful campus and let me ask questions. Jean Monnet, though, is a completely fictional institution (sadly). Thank you to Hisham Wyne for Lahore intel; thanks also to Aoibhlinn Hester-Wyne.

As ever, my biggest thank-you goes to Alex: for telling me I can do it, for cheering me on, and for meeting me at the finish line with ice cream.

Juno's about to discover there's nothing
more scary than falling in love . . .

Available now

Nicola grew up in Monkstown, Co. Dublin before moving
to London after university. She worked in publishing for
several years before writing her first book, *The Out of Office
Girl*, which was shortlisted for the RNA Romantic Novel of
the Year 2013. Her second book, *If I Could Turn Back
Time*, was published by Headline in 2014 and her third
book *Girls on Tour* is available as a series of ebook shorts
and in print. Nicola lives in Highbury, north London, with
her husband and no cats (yet).

nicoladohertybooks.com